wasp in the opium flowers

Also by Kevin Klix:

wasp in the opium flowers

kevin klix

klix Artwork LTD. | Est. 2009

for **Brandon Wanless**

NO LIVES MATTER. Copyright © 2017 by Kevin Klix.
WASP IN THE OPIUM FLOWERS. Copyright © 2018 by Kevin Klix. All rights reserved. Printed in the United States of America. No part of this publication may be reproduced, distributed, or transmitted in any form or by any means, or stored in a database or retrieval system, without the prior written permission from the author. For information about permission to reproduce sections from this book, email to Permissions, Kevin Klix, at kevinklix@yahoo.com.

SECOND EDITION

Designed by Kevin Klix

Library of Congress Cataloguing-in-Publication Date is available upon request.

Type set in New Baskerville LT / Titles set in Helvetica Neue

ISBN: 978-0-9965410-6-0

14 13 12 11 10 / 10 9 8 7 6 5 4 3 2 1

"An alert reader will have noticed a gaping hole in our last proof of Algorithm E, however. We never showed that the algorithm terminates; all we have proved is that *if* it terminates, it gives the right answer! (Notice, for example, that Algorithm E still makes sense if we allow its variables m, n, c, and r to assume values of the form $u + v \sqrt{2}$, where u and v are integers. The variables q, a, b, a', b' are to remain integer-valued. If we start the algorithm with $m = 12 - 6 \sqrt{2}$ and $n = 20 - 10 \sqrt{2}$, say, it will compute a "greatest common divisor" $d = 4 - 2 \sqrt{2}$ with $a = +2$, b = -1. Even under this extension of the assumptions, the proofs of assertions *A1* through *A6* remain valid; therefore all assertions are true throughout any execution of the algorithm. But if we start the procedure with $m = 1$ and $n = 4$ the computation never terminates (see exercise 12). Hence a proof of assertions *A1* through *A6* does not logically prove that the algorithm is finite.) Proofs of termination are usually handled separately. But exercise 13 shows that it is possible to extend the method above in many important cases so that a proof of termination is included as a by-product."

— Donald E. Knuth,
The Art of Computer Programming, Third Edition

"I enjoy wasting the reader's time with all my 1,000-pagers."

— Not an actual quote from Stephen King

contents

introduction

KEVIN KLIX IS A LUNATIC. He's a womanizer. He likes to do things specifically just to upset people. Kevin once bragged to me about being a *professional internet troll.* I swear to *nonexistent God,* five of the top ten strangest things I've ever heard anyone say, has come out of Kevin's mouth. He once told me he likes a chick to fuck him like he's not even in the room, not looking at him or paying any attention to him. He said that's what gets him off. When I asked why, he told me, *I like to see how they experience pleasure when they're alone.* Weird. I told him at that point he might as well just stalk them, watch them through their blinds. He replied with, *Nah, that's creepy.* I'm constantly at a loss for words being Kevin's actual friend. But sometimes I think maybe he's on to something. Maybe he understands people on a fundamental level, a basic level. Sure, maybe Kevin is just a self-serving asshole. But maybe not. Maybe he just learned how to cut through all the bullshit and self-doubt that haunts us as humans by asking himself one question: *Who cares?*

What matters in this life? Is it getting a desk job that provides insurance and paid sick days? Is it falling in love and marrying a woman who understands you and accepts you for who you are? Is it having kids and raising them to be a better human than you? The answer is no. And yes. But in actually, the answer really doesn't matter. None of it does. There is no formula. And there is no set path in life. We're all just atoms and stardust floating around in the ether.

And that's where it starts. Nihilism. The first time this concept was presented to me it was with a tone of disdain, drenched in negative connotation. It's a concept for people who don't care about life. Wrong. I realized that it was a concept for people who understood that nothing in this life truly matters. Meaning is merely just mental designation. Morals are something we create for ourselves. They're malleable. We create the world we live in. There are no rules.

This realization is the most freeing experience I've had in my entire life. It's the beauty in nihilism. When you realize that nothing matters you understand that there's nothing holding you back. There's no reason to be scared or intimidated anymore. Life becomes your sandbox. Play with everything and have fun.

It's the arbitrary beauty of our lives. How they intersect. Sometimes we're given these moments that are hot and sticky, raw and weird. Sometimes our experiences are quick and cool, effortless and deep. But every single day we wake up and the only thing that keeps us going is the promise of connection. In one form or another that's our greatest high. We're always chasing the dragon.

Even when we know we're addicted, especially when it comes to women, we can't help ourselves. We try and try, beat our heads against walls in frustration, scream and cry, trying to fight the urge of urge itself. But, why? Why continue to fight against something that lives in our soul? The human angst. Unrest. The urge to go out there and meet new people. Let people go. There is no guideline on how to live a happy life. It's something we feel inside of ourselves and have to navigate on our own.

And that's what NO LIVES MATTER* is, a story about the guy who stopped fighting that urge. On the surface we see Steven, our protagonist, the ultimate fuckboy. This guy is by all means a certified Grade-A douchebag. But there's something noble in the way he lives his life. Some people would call it cockiness. It's not. It's not quite confidence either. It's this strange middle ground, this moral limbo, Steven chooses to operate within. He's not a liar. But he's not exactly honest either. Steven has created his own rules to live his life by: If it feels good, do it. If it doesn't, then don't.

Our protagonist isn't this scary, jaded pessimistic dickhead. He's brave beyond reason. He gets very little out of social interaction. Especially with women. In fact, he sees women as a hindrance. He loves everything about them, physically. But when it comes to actually interacting with them, it's a chore. It's a chore that he continues to torture himself with. Even after finding the perfect woman, he still finds himself wondering about his ex and his previous hookups and still reaches out. It's an endless cycle. It's all fleeting. It's all pointless. So reach out. Or be an asshole. Do what makes you fucking happy.

------

* Published as WASP IN THE OPIUM FLOWERS as of May, 2018

That's honestly the best advice ever given to me. We're all here on this planet for a very short moment. My buddy Jake says, Whatever man, I'm gonna be dead longer than I'm alive. That is one of the most comforting sentiments I've heard in my life. He has no idea where he stole it from, but it's a phrase that comes to mind often. Everything is so fleeting. Our lives, our relationships, things we find to be important. It just doesn't make sense to tie ourselves down to anything for too long. Find the noble honesty in living your life selfishly. That's where personal solace lies. In our passion, our desires, our addictions. We're all narcissists. We're all addicts. We're all trapped here together in the now. Smile and enjoy gravity. And as Steven might say, Don't be a little bitch.

So I'm sure this isn't the introduction Kevin wanted. In fact, I think he might be pissed I didn't make him look like a complete and total fuck-head. Sorry bro, I actually liked your novel. This is my introduction, and I'm the king of my domain. Fuck you.

Fictional character in this novel[†],
Scott Casey Geller
June 1, 2017

[†] A message to the reader from Kevin Klix: "Scott Geller is an actual real person, people. I swear. He's just trolling me."

wasp in the
opium flowers

one

YOU IMAGINE RAILING THE HOLE of a smooth Slovakian hardbody of about twenty-one years of age. Though this is on your mind, you can't help but think of your girlfriend, Janne. Her looks can be described by this action: She brings you the complimentary Starbucks every morning at about 8- or 9- o'clock when she graciously knocks on your downtown apartment door located near the Publix on Rosemary Street, downtown West Palm Beach, Florida. You think of Janne and how she does this act and what goes through her mind. Could it be that she loves you? Could it be that she wants to marry you? Could it be that she values you as a man? None of these things seem to pop into your head because, again, you're thinking about railing the hole of a smooth, twenty-something Slovakian hardbody, and Janne seems to be irrelevant at this moment.

Your phone whistles the urge shrill of bells and you pull it out of your pocket as you're sitting down bored out of your mind on your living-room couch. You look down at your screen to see you have received a message on your Tinder app. You click passed the message and go straight to this potential hardbody's profile to see it's a black woman, 24, lips thin, eyes a bright, bright contact-colored green, the curve of her ass seemingly wider than the length of her waist, the black & white striped shirt she's wearing that's probably bought from somewhere local at some thrift store—maybe the Goodwill on Dixie Highway or something of that sort. She's sexy but appears to be the kind of woman that likes a guy who can spend more than he earns on just her so she can latch her greasy paws on him forever and take half his net worth. . . . So obviously you approve and go back to your inbox to see that her message reads:

Brittany: Hey.

This is pretty standard for women on dating sites, especially one as superficial as Tinder, but no matter, this further fuels your theory of her gold-digging tendencies. So you message her back:

You: Um, hey too. Where did you get that shirt? I like the stripes. It accentuates your figure very nicely.

You type this and read it over before clicking send. Should you put a heart or smiley-face at the end of it? No. That seems particularly lame and only someone—or some lame guy, or whatever—would actually have the gall to place an emoji at the end of his compliment, making the female in question receiving it conclude that he is a "nice guy" and wants to gain her approval and ultimately date her and care for her and maybe even buy her random Starbucks in the mornings for her to look for other male prospects elsewhere, ones that are dominant, "confident," as some females put, and doesn't have a care in the world about anything but knowing—without a shadow of a doubt—that they are "the shit" and nothing can stop them.

As you're thinking all of this, you notice that you hadn't even once considered the notion of looking up at what her name is—though it doesn't really matter on a mindless exchange such as this: You look and see "Brittany." You lightly laugh in the back of your throat at the name because it reminds you of a slut-whore's name somewhere in the recesses of your memory. You think of a petite white chick, probably 19-ish, slut-ing around in her mini-skirt, taking shots left and right at the club and screaming, "Fuck yeah!! A-L-C-O-H-O-L! Fuck *yeah!*" and wishing one day, when she's in her late thirties, that she will eventually marry a wealthy man, have children with him, live in a nice suburban home near the beach or Intracoastal, and drink tea and read pointless romance novels with her reading group after her nonexistent job ends. You think of this and the name "Brittany" together and then shake your head and realize that this is probably bias assumptions. You click send.

You are hungry. So you stand up, stretch, and walk to the kitchen. There is a note on the counter that reads: "Left you last night's din din in the fridge. Love you! XOXO" in curvy, bold, pink, handwritten scrawl. Last night you had McDonald's when Janne came over, so you squint your eyes and shake your head at the stupidity of this note—because obviously Janne made it to give you a sense of comfort or approval of her to make you think of her as a sweet, kind, gentle woman—almost motherly, maybe-probably—and how her awesome, cute font looks on a napkin that lays atop your kitchen counter, and the "effort" it took to write it before she left this morning (as you remind her time and time again to do, the leaving of your personal dojo). You crumble up the note, vaguely having this burning sensation in the pit of your stomach that you can't seem to shake, and you toss it in the trashcan, hoping that she never, ever notices by some off chance that you threw her note away. Nevertheless, you're hungry, so you open the fridge. A McDonald's bag.

With it in hand, you sit at the table. There are cigarette butts on top, scattered about. You can't really remember if it was yours or Janne's because of the fact that you drank a little bit too much before Janne came over the night before; it's hard to pinpoint which from when. No matter, you assume it was the both of you and pile them all up together with the intent on throwing them away later. You open the McDonald's bag. Cold fries and a 10-piece box of chicken nuggets with only 3 nuggets left inside it, and an opened BBQ sauce beside the 3 with a thin layer of hardened crust at the top of it. . . . It's food though. You shouldn't be greedy. You should think of the starving children in Africa who would give anything to be in your position, in America, white male, tall, reasonably handsome, light scruff on the face, vaguely long, curly hair, and a modest fashion style of T-shirts, Levis, and Converse Chuck Taylor's. Or having the IQ of a serial-killing, rapist-like, bigoted, atheist–conservative—a strange but rare combination, you're aware of—and be able to read books at about 900 words-per-minute with prolific and clear retainment of about 85%. But it doesn't matter. You scarf down the fries and leave the chicken nuggets for your beautiful doggie, Sparky.

You set down the nuggets on the floor and immediately dopey Sparky comes running up, his paws scurrying and almost slipping under themselves as if he's almost falling (though he never does). "Come here, boy!" you say to him in a very squeaky, cheerful voice. "I love you! Sparky, *boy!* Come get the *food!*" He starts eating aggressively, licking the ground under where ("underwear") they once were and he looks up with his big, beady, dough eyes and he has his long, pink, wet tongue out, drooling and panting because of how excited he is. You think of him and his life: All he wants to do is gain any standard of pleasure. It's an animal. It's a dog. It's a living creature that wants food, sex, sleep, and to put in the least amount of work into their life as possible. Besides sex—which you frankly wouldn't mind condoning, but would require you to let him run free which would (a) Create huge problems with the city's pound, (b) Someone taking him and naming him something like "Spot" or "Rover," or (c) Have him gain some kind of weird health problem; not from the sex *itself* but from being out in the streets—you honestly believe that you provide him with at least three of those four things so, in essence, he's about 75% happy with his existence. That, you're afraid, is all you can hope for. "Good boy, Sparky!" you say, playfully petting him. He licks your hands.

Your phone whistles a tone again and you look down to see that you got a new message on Tinder. It's about 8:05 A.M. on a Saturday. You wonder who in the world would be messaging you back at this time. Then you remember the black hardbody named Brittany and you quickly swipe the message open. . . . You read it over, it says:

Brittany: Hey! Thanks for noticing! I actually got the shirt from my church I go to. They always have people donating the coolest stuff. I volunteer, so yeah.

Well, that's all great information. She volunteers and is a church girl—and obviously is black. You don't want to be stereotypical but you assume she is probably a freak in the bedroom, so you message her back. But right before you are about to click send, there is a knock at your front door. You look up, lock your phone, and walk toward it. You twist the knob and open.

"Hey, Steve!"

It's Janne.

"Got you Starbucks," she says.

"Yeah," you say. "Thanks, babe." You wave her in.

Janne plants a kiss on your cheek, hands you your drink, and parades on in. You close the door behind her. You think of slapping her ass as she walks in to showcase your dominance—and maybe your need for sex—but then you realize that you are well passed those types of petty exchanges. Janne is fully aware of your intents.

"Stevie," Janne says, pointing at the table.

"What?" you say.

"You just leave your trash on the table and all your cigarette butts in a pile and not even care about it? What's wrong with you?"

You pause. "Sorry . . . ?"

She smiles. "Just be more mindful." She kneels under your sink and grabs a roll of paper-towels—probably the same ones she wrote her note with—and a blue bottle of Windex. She stands up and walks over to the table and squirts the liquid all over the pile of cigarette butts, making a nice, thick paste, and wipes it off the edge of the table and onto her cupped hand. She drops it all into the McDonald's bag and finally throws the bag full of crap away in the trash. She looks over at you and says, "Steve, you really gotta stop smoking. You're killing yourself."

You laugh and say, "But you smoke too!"

She rolls her eyes. "I quit yesterday. Remember?"

"Oh. I guess so." You don't because you were too drunk and you honestly don't give a rat's ass about her health choices . . . or any of her personal choices for that matter.

You take a sip of your caramel macchiato and notice that it tastes less sweet. "Um, what is *this* shit?"

"Stevie, it's skim milk."

"The fuck is 'skim milk'?" You know perfectly good and well what skim milk is, but you know that Janne knows that she shouldn't mess with your coffee or deter from the normal set of requirements for your highly-caffeinated beverage.

She says, "I think it's better for you. I want you to make good choices, like me. Gotta start taking care of yourself."

You take a sip and think, furthermore, how little you care about her personal choices, but for her to impose those choices on you and dictate what you should and shouldn't do is absolutely preposterous to you. Nevertheless, you say, "Thanks, babe. Thanks for caring about me so much."

She smiles, steps forward, and you two start making-out. You're hoping that this will extend further into something, so you, at the same time sucking her face, shimmy you and her both toward the kitchen table and set your "skim milk" Starbucks on top of it. You start groping her ass and lifting her up. She obliges and lifts her leg and you lift it up further. You grab her other leg, the back of her thigh, and she lifts that one, too. She his hugging your shoulders tight. You continue to make-out. You start walking towards the bedroom. You kick your slightly-opened door and it swings outwardly open, making it appear like you're actually strong—but in actuality, you're really just showing off. Janne stops kissing you and says, "Oh *my!* Someone's an eager-beaver." She giggles. You could care less, you just want her to get naked. You toss her onto your bed. She giggles again and starts taking off her T-shirt. You pull your T-shirt off, too, and throw it somewhere, anywhere, off in Non-Sex Land.

You pull your jeans down, not wearing any boxers. You vaguely remember Janne and her telling you she hates it when you "go commando," and how much she wishes that you would wear the boxers that she bought you for Christmas a couple months ago (that you have never opened and is in the dresser that—oh, *look!*—your shirt you just tossed is hanging over).

You remember this and look in Janne's eyes and see that it doesn't vaguely upset her, but she doesn't want to be a bitch about it and kill the mood so she doesn't say anything. This is basically the exact reason why you desire sex so much. In the bedroom, a male is always king, you think. He's the boss. He runs the show. And females seem to love it. They want their love interest to take charge and do whatever they desire to them—within cautious reason, of course. One will not simply consent to sexual intercourse of a weird nature: such as beating her with five dead rattlesnakes or some other weird, and frankly obnoxious, sexual act that you only see in fetish snuff films online. You think of this and grin, and Janne grins too. She pulls her skirt down and you think of imaginary "Brittany."

You're naked, Janne is just in her red Victoria's Secret panties that you bought last year for Valentine's day just for this specific sight to occur. You climb on top of her, sucking her face, grabbing her C-cup ta-tas aggressively, and she curls, contorts backward, and moans, "Baby . . ." You move your hand downward and into her panties. You place your index and middle finger on her clit and press down on it and spin in slow, small circles. She moans, "Ah, fuck yes. . . . *Yes!*" You insert your middle finger slowly inside her hole and slowly pull out and reinsert. This appears to make her go crazy. So you do it faster and start sucking on her right nipple. You aren't even hard yet; this is just, to you, careless routine sex. Janne grabs your wrist, looks into your eyes, and says, "Fuck me, please." You pull down her panties and you can feel your cock rising, erecting, blood rushing a million miles-per-hour inside of it, to the tip. Flushing the veins and swelling your testicles with pure ecstasy. And you're not even there yet.

Fuck it. You toss her panties over your shoulder, just like

your T-shirt, and hope it lands on it. You vaguely want it to, so her drippings can soak kind of into the shirt itself and you can lick and smell it later in the bathroom while you masturbate to Mia Khalifa sucking cock on PornHub. You feel Janne's hole one more time and notice how soaked she is. She's ready. You say, "I'm gonna fuck you hard, you little slut." You look at her and her eyes kind of widen at that phrase, as if you don't say this shit all the time to her (which, frankly, you do). You think of her being told as a child or teenager about rapists and the weird shit they say, and how this sentence is probably one of those weird things. But at this point, you're the man and she's in your room, soaking wet, naked—*both* of you naked, actually —so you can do literally anything and say anything you want. . . . Obviously.

Janne says, "Yes, Daddy," and pulls you toward herself. You start kissing her. She strangely is kissing you in a very sweet, careful sort of way, as if she is trying to "make love" to you. You don't give a fuck about that shit. You insert your tongue into her mouth and massage her tongue with it. This quickly makes her forget about a romantic kind of sex. She pulls you closer. You stop, look down, and see your cock rock hard and about to be inserted into her warm, wet hole. You see no condom on and thank nonexistent *God* that Janne is on birth control. It's actually one of the perks of having a regular, steady girlfriend, you think. You grab your cock, look back into Janne's eyes, and she has this look on her face. It's this bashful, coy look. It almost makes you want to punish it, destroy it, and make it stop. So you plunge your cock inside her and she lets out a "Fuck! *Ahhh,* fuck yeah!! Fuck, *baby!* Fuck!!" You start pumping her hard and deep, as fast as you can, no slow, dramatic intros needed.

"FUCK, FUCK!! STEVEN!!! FUCK!! *SHIT!*" Janne is

moaning and you're just going to town. You're making quick, wet slapping sounds from her hips being crashed into by your hips repeatedly. You grope her tits and start making-out with her. She has her arms around your back, pulling you close. You want to fuck her the way that you always want to fuck her: you lean back, on your knees, and grab both her legs and push them all the way back, basically her knees to her ears, exposing her pink lips as they swell with your cock inside. You hold her legs back and leverage yourself so you can start pumping. You slam her pussy, jack-hammering as quickly as possible, not even looking at her, just staring at the headboard. She's moaning and repeating "Yes!" and "Fuck me harder!" and then finally says, "Cum on my face!"

For some weird reason, her saying to "cum on her face" turns you off slightly. You don't really know why that is. Maybe it's because she brought you Starbucks and that very act alone is un-slut-like, and the sound of her saying these words makes her a backdoor-slut, which makes it less spontaneous. You never mind that and keep pumping away. You pump for what seems to be forever. Finally, her moans turn to silence and she says, "Baby . . . ?"

You stop.

"What?"

"Can you fuck me slow?"

"Uh, yeah, sure." So you start going slow but deep. You pull her close, legs still basically back. Then she wraps them around you.

She says, "I love you, baby. Cum inside me, please."

Did she change her mind? This takes you off kilter. You pull out (not listening to her request—because fuck her, right?) and spray 8 white ropes all over her stomach and tits. You would have came inside her but instinct tells you to not trust any woman with your seed, even if she does take any form of contraceptive(s). You say, shaking, gripping your cock, "Fuhhh*hhhhhhh-ck!* Yes!"—last of the drops—"Yup. Fuck yeah. Cool." You roll off her and lay on your back. You say, "That was *real* fuckin' great." You can see the fan spinning above you. You feel the air and notice how sweaty you are. *How can women enjoy the sweat of men?* you think. You stand up beside your side of the bed, walk to the dresser, grab your T-shirt—and additionally notice Janne's panties on the ground and not on the shirt itself, like you had hoped—and toss the shirt over to her and say, "Here. Wipe yourself off."

Still lying down, she grabs the shirt, nods, and wipes off her stomach and tits off. When she is satisfied with the cleanup, she tosses it into your laundry hamper, where all the other yellowed, more crusty shirts are. You say, "Fuck, I need to do laundry." Janne doesn't say anything to that. She just closes her eyes and grabs your pillow and covers herself. Janne is beautiful when she does this, you think. Besides how much you despise being in a relationship, these are some of the perks. You sit beside her and eventually notice her breathing softens and slows down and she finally falls fast asleep. You look down at your wet, flaccid cock and feel proud of it. You cup your balls and pull upward and you laugh because as a kid you always imagined your cock looking exactly like the head of a fly: the balls the hexagon-webbed eyes, the cock the stinger.

You stand up, pull up your jeans from the ground passed your legs and zip yourself up. You walk out into the kitchen and stand there. You think of "Brittany" and what maybe her pussy would feel like. You pull out and unlock your phone and can see your Tinder message that you meant to send out to her still waiting there. It says:

You: Yeah. I go to church too. I support anybody who
       helps out people in need. 😃

After careful, thoughtful pleasantries, Brittany appears to approve of you when she types you her cellphone number and permits you to give her a text instead of messaging on "that pesky Tinder chat," as she so calls it. You concur, save her number, open up your iMessage application.

Walk to the couch.

Plop down.

Start texting the black slut.

two

You: Hey, what's up? It's Steve from Tinder. You can put my last name as "Tinder," because we both know that's what's gonna be done!

Brittany Tinder: Cool! Haha, yeah. That's fine. I do that anyways! So it says you're a writer on your account? Is that right?

You: Yeah. I dabble.

Brittany Tinder: Cool! What do you write about?

You: It's hard to explain. Basically I take the worst subjects of all time and just exploit them to the world.

Brittany Tinder: That's cool. My brother writes poems n stuff. Have you written any books?

You: A few. Mostly fiction. I just write whatever I'm into at the time. But yeah, all my books are related to each other. So that's cool.

Brittany Tinder: Wow! You're like creative as heck!

Brittany Tinder: That's super cute! 😀

You: Thanks.

wasp in the opium flowers

You: So what are you getting into today?

Brittany Tinder: I have no clue honestly, I just kind of got up early and checked my phone and got on Tinder n stuff. Swiped right on you and now here we are!

You: Sounds lovely. 😴 Glad I made the cut. You're hot.

Brittany Tinder: Thanks! You're not too bad yourself! Sooo why did you get on Tinder?

You: Basically I'm newly single. And I wanted to have some fun and shop around.

Brittany Tinder: Shop around? You sound like a player! 😡 Shame on you!

You: Nah, it's not like that. I talk to one girl at a time. It's just hard to find chicks worth my time. Are you worth it?

Brittany Tinder: Babe, please! I'm kickass! I graduated with a degree in business, I'm responsible, easy on the eyes, and I drive a crappy Honda Accord.

You: Sounds like a winner to me! 😴 What kind of food are you into?

Brittany Tinder: I basically just like anything. What do you like?

You: I like mostly Italian food. Like pizza and shit like that.

Brittany Tinder: That's cool. Why are you up so early anyhow?

You: Bored. Woke up just like you and decided to go swiping right basically.

Brittany Tinder: Sooo let me ask. Are you one of those guys that just swipes right on every girl you see?

You: Haha. What do YOU think? 😒

Brittany Tinder: 😶 Oh dear! Another one.

You: It's not a bad thing. Guys that only swipe right simply are saying that it's up to the girls to decide. I do swipe left if it's absolutely an unbearable chick to look at.

Brittany Tinder: Soo you care about looks huh?

You: Don't we all?

Brittany Tinder: I guess. I just care about what's on the inside. I was raised traditionally and I want a good husband one day.

You: Yeah. So was I. I'm a total gentleman. I make sure women are taken care of.

Brittany Tinder: Really?? 😄 You're so sweet!

You: Hell yeah I is! Booya!

Brittany Tinder: And funny..

You: So what you got going on today? Any plans?

Brittany Tinder: Ummm no. Not really. Why?

You: Basically I'm seeing if you want to eat pizza with a fucking handsome devil. And it's on me. So free food is always cool. You down or what?

Brittany Tinder: Yeah but we just met basically. Isn't that unsafe?

You: So? I'm harmless, you're harmless. Let's do something. I think it'll be kickass.

You: We'll just go downtown Lake Worth and eat at that Downtown Pizza place.

wasp in the opium flowers

Brittany Tinder: Yeah sure! Sounds fun. 😊 When do you want to go?

You: In about an hour.

Brittany Tinder: Okay good. I want to get ready.

You: Eh, you don't have to. Dress casual. Just T-shirt and some jeans. That's all I'm gonna wear.

Brittany Tinder: Really? Woah! You're sweeter than I thought! Now I don't have to stress about it.

You: Hey. That's what I'm here for, babe. Um, where do you stay at?

Brittany Tinder: I actually live close to downtown Lake Worth.

You: What intersection?

Brittany Tinder: I don't want to say.. In case you're a creeper. No offense.

You: None taken. Okay. In an hour meet me at Downtown Pizza. I'll give you the address.

Brittany Tinder: Cool. See you then, cutie. 😜

You: 7█ ████████ Ave, L██████ W████, FL ██████

three

GRINNING EAR TO EAR, YOU'RE STARING DOWN at your phone and wondering how many times you've done this same spiel to every woman you have ever come across. Not just to Brittany but to Janne as well; the number of times are uncountable that you have lied to another human being just to get your sick, sadistic pleasures fulfilled—whatever they may be, even if you aren't consciously aware of them. The high school chicks you dated in your teen years . . . the chicks you have come across in bars and giving zero drinks to . . . the dates of every woman you have ever met were all phony fabrications of the ideal man specifically designed for her needs and desires ("her" being whatever woman at the time). You simply lie; that's all you're good at. You grin, stand, and notice a random shirt crumbled and wrinkled up on the ground. You walk toward it, lean down, pick it up, and put it on; you know it looks like shit, but frankly, Brittany doesn't seem like that kind of girl to put any effort into. You go into your bedroom.

That sleeping girl. You lean forward, your mouth hovering over her ear. "Joanne . . ." you whisper, "I'm going out for awhile." She doesn't appear to have woken up. She vaguely nods a yes at you and says a "have fun." You say, "I love you," and she says, "I love you, too." All seems perfect as you stand back out into your living-room and think of the possibility of having sexual intercourse with a lovely stripe-wearing, black, hardbody, Christian bitch from Tinder you're about to spend virtually no money on for a slice of pizza, good conversation, and possibly coax her into everything she wants on this one single date. You grab your keys on the stand that holds up your television and walk out your front door. You get into your car. Key in ignition, pull out, drive, drive, drive. . . .

You eventually drive southbound down Dixie Highway and coast a measly 35 miles-per-hour while listening to the latest popular music on the radio. You click a station; one is rap, pop, and new-age hip-hop; one is alternative, one is techno, one is something you can't pinpoint. You eventually land on 104.3 The Shark and listen to Ashley O and Toast on "The Big Mistake," their morning talk-show. They are talking about a potato chip that is supposedly the hottest chip in the world with the hottest pepper: "The Carolina Reaper." They are discussing how they want to purchase one and try it out on their show, or on the show's Facebook live. They want the audience to tell them where they can find this chip because it isn't in the south Florida area anywhere. They may have to order it online, they say. Oh well, you think.

You look down this road and continue to coast your way, almost approaching downtown Lake Worth, and you see a bum on the street. For all of 5 seconds, you glance at him and notice his scraggly hair, his unshaven, butchered face, his shoes clearly given to him from Shoes For Crews, a company specifically designed to cater to bartenders, servers, and pretty much anyone in the food industry. *What a guy!* you think. Here's this bum, possibly not even an American citizen (stereotyping), who is down on his luck by the sheer negligence of the world around him that is beyond his control;

everything this man knows is clearly a failure as he stands on the cement median and stares blankly at the cars passing, hoping that in one interval of a stop light he gets the chance to take money from people who know how hard the world is and know what it means to make a single buck. He looks like he's hustling. You have seen this a thousand, million times in your town; every intersection seems to have a bum on it, maybe even 2 or 3. You don't know why you're looking at this bum and why he bothers you so much, but it (he) does, as you drive past him in your car, a vehicle you're privileged enough to own and use for your supposed necessities. And this bum has nothing but hope that he doesn't die of starvation.

The intersection of Dixie and Lucerne Avenue is quickly coming up ahead, and you're thinking about how early you are to be here. You decide to take a left and see yourself at your favorite bar, where you always pregame. *It's early,* you think, *but fuck it, why not?* Life is too short to have to conform to all of the normalcies expected of you from a cold, selfish society. You think of Ayn Rand's *Atlas Shrugged* and of her philosophy: Objectivism. It comes into your bleak mind and eventually you get lost in the concept of selfishness and how truly awesome it is. You parallel park your car. The music is playing some song by Weezer or The Struts, or some other band that sounds exactly like Twenty One Pilots. You have heard the songs a million, zillion times and for some apparent reason it still makes you nod and bob your head, despite you never looking up the song itself and adding it to your iTunes library on your personal computer at home. You know Janne would love these songs, and maybe has even heard them before. You think all this and drone on and don't even realize that you're now at the bar, one you have no clue what the name is, but nothing matters, nothing truly, completely matters. Thoughts are here and there and control every moment of your existence.

You wave your hand at the bartender and take a seat on the stool. You say, "Hey, buddy!" The guy turns around, and you notice it isn't a guy; it's just a woman that has short hair and dresses in men's clothing. She actually looks cute. She has a weird tattoo of an ox on her neck. She walks toward you.

"Hey, sweetie—what d'you wanna drink?"

You grin. "Anything that makes me forget."

"One of those days, huh?"

"Of course."

"I'll just give you a Bud Light. How's that?"

You're thinking how bad it tastes and can't help but consciously make a look on your face.

"No, huh?" the bartender says, clearly noticing your disdain. "Um, whiskey then?"

You ask, "Do you have PBR?"

"Yeah—of course. It's in a can, though."

"It's going down the same place. Hit me."

The bartender nods and kneels down to the fridge in front of her, pulls up a beer, pops open the can, and says, "Shit."

"What?" you say.

"I literally just opened this and didn't look for your I.D."

"I'm old enough."

"How old?"

"Old enough to party." You wink.

The bartender rolls her eyes and says, "Yeah, like I never heard *that* before. Whatever—you just drink your beer. If you need me, I'll be here."

"Stick around. Let's talk."

"Yeah, sure. One caveat though."

"Yeah . . . ?"

"I just gotta clean my spoons."

"Yeah, do your thing."

The bartender grabs a rag a couple feet away, on the other side of the bar, and also grabs a big grey tub full of utensils. She sets it beside you. She says, "Sorry. Hope you don't mind."

"Not at all. I do have a question though," you say.

"Hm?"

"What's that tattoo mean?"

The bartender smiles. "Oh, *this*. It's a long story."

"I got nothing but time, babe." You take a hit of your beer. "Go on."

"Well, my father is Chinese; I'm Buddhist. It's like a symbol of servitude in our culture. I got it because it reminds me of him and I. Once we were gardening and he was showing me all these plants, and this rabbit came. He was saying a rabbit is the polar opposite of an ox. An ox is basically a castrated bull. So it's kind of a hard knock life. And a rabbit literally just reproduces like crazy and leeches off anything and everything it can find . . . That's what my father said, anyway. So it kind of stuck with me. So I turned 16 and got this tattoo. It's a little bit faded but it's okay still; I'm glad it still looks like an actual ox." She laughs. "It's just a pretty cool ox. I like it. It's just more personal to me. Do you have any tattoos, Mr. . . ."

"My name's Steve."

"Oh okay. You got any tats, Stevie?"

"Just Steve. I hate Stevie."

"Sorry . . ."

"I don't really have tattoos at all. I've never wanted one."

"Why? It's super fun."

"I just don't like needles."

"Oh, what a pussy!"

"Come on," you laugh. "Give me a break!"

"I'm just giving you shit. Men never handle pain very well."

"Yeah. We're all pussies. What's funny is women are clearly better than men."

"*Ha!* Why's that?"

"For one, women only have a finite amount of eggs while men have a virtually endless amount. There really doesn't need to be that many men in this world. We're all hairy, gross, always thinking about some sexual shit . . . and it's just not needed. You literally only need, like, at minimum, one guy for every million chicks. It's science."

"Yeah, but dick is great, though."

"Hey! I ain't knockin' ya, sweetheart. I just would love to be the one guy out of the million girls. I would have insane amounts of girlfriends."

"You're a player, huh?"

"Sort of. I just think all women are beautiful. I wish all of them could be my girlfriend."

"You wouldn't want that. We're all nuts."

"We all got our flaws. But even then chicks can have sex with chicks and still be straight. Guys can't do that. Shit, we can't even *cry* without being laughed at. Being a dude is the worst."

"Well," the bartender shrugs, "at least you're not a lame feminist."

You laugh. "I'm a Meninist."

"*Ha!* Wow! Ain't never heard *that* before."

"I want men to have equal rights!" you joke, "I want the women to spend the equal amount I spend on the ring I give her—it's only fair game. The guy has to spend money, the guy has to make all the choices. Shit, the guy is the one that has to lead in the bedroom. You can't even show vulnerability until you're actually in a relationship. It's lame as hell!"

"That's just odd to think about. Women aren't that superficial."

"The hot ones are. If you literally think about it, these chicks are looked at all the time, catered to all the time, and they are constantly praised and bombarded with compliments."

"Eh, I don't know . . ."—bartender scratching head—"I'm not that hot and I get hit-on all the time."

You laugh. "No dude, you *are* hot."

"Really? You think so?" She smirks.

"Yeah, of course. I mean, I don't really like your shirt and pants. But other than that you're, like, a solid 8."

"I mean, yeah, thanks, but I'm at work. I'm not really trying to attract guys."

"How about I get a kiss?"

"Wha' . . . ?"

"A kiss!"

"Babe, I'm married."

"Yeah? Where's your ring?"

"Home."

"Ah, come on!" You lean in. You get 90 percent of the way there and she goes the remainder 10 percent and you both do a little pecker kiss—nothing big. Afterward, you say, "That was cool."

The bartender laughs and says, "Yeah, that was fun."

You laugh too. "So, um, what's your name?"

"Smooth. Very smooth. I'm Natalie. You can call me Nat, though. Like pronounced 'gnat.' Those crappy little bugs."

"At least you're not a shitty wasp. You're a cuddle bug! You basically just lay back and have fun, huh?"

"With my husband, yes."

"Oh shit. You actually have a husband, for real? I thought you were just joking. My bad, yo. For the kiss."

"It's cool. I liked it." Nat finishes wiping off the last of her utensils and has them in a fairly large pile next to her. She says, "Cool, I'm done." She grabs all of them and puts them back into the grey tub. She walks back to the other side of the bar and sets the tub on top of the counter. She walks back but, before she even gets to you, she asks, "Want another PBR?"

You look down. Your beer is empty. You don't remember taking that many sips. Time slipped by. You look up and say, "Yeah, sure. But how did you know it was empty?"

"The condensation bubbles are all gone from the sides. Insider trick of the trade, baby!" Nat leans down and pulls out another beer for you. She opens it, places it in front of you, takes your empty can and tosses it away in the trashcan next to her. She turns back to you, asks, "So why are you here so early?"

You look around. "Yeah. You're probably wondering why I'm such a weirdo, sitting here alone in your bar, in the early morning basically. I don't know why I'm here. I'm supposed to meet a chick from Tinder soon."

Nat leans back, eye-rolling so hard. "Tinder? You're not, like, one of *those* guys, are you?"

"Huh?"

"You know, you just go on dates and have sex with chicks."

"I mean, isn't that what Tinder is meant to be used for?"

"Yeah. That's true. Is this chick cute?"

"Yeah. I'll show you." You pull out your phone, click your Tinder app and open up Brittany's profile. You swipe to her most attractive photo and flash it to Nat. You say, "She's cute."

Nat grabs your phone. "Yeah. I like her. She's sweet. I like her wardrobe."

"The stripes are lovely."

"Yeah, I love it." Nat hands your phone back to you. "So what is she into? What does she do?"

You laugh. "I don't know. I'm just trying to fuck her. There's not any real point in trying to get to know her."

"I guess so. Well . . . if it makes you happy . . . Nothing I can argue about."

You lean back and chug the rest of your second PBR. You slam the empty can down on the counter and say, "Third one?"

Nat nods. "Sure." She kneels down and grabs a third from the fridge and places it in front of you. This time you take your empty can and toss it yourself into the trashcan next to Nat. She says, "Thanks."

"No sweat."

"So, uh, when are you meeting her?"

"I don't know. Like 15-minutes or something. We're eating at Downtown Pizza."

"Great place. Love it. Say Nat sent you. The owner and I are cool. He'll give you the hookup."

"Great. Free food and free pussy." You laugh. "Just kidding."

"You're not." Nat laughs. This is totally awk. "You're so man-ish."

"Man-ish? *The fuck is that,* man-*ish?*"

"You know, Steve, like basically you're just a barbarian or something. Into only sex and beer. Do you like sports?"

"I don't know. Kind of. I like the Broncos. But it's basically all my friends do."

"Yeah, they're a good team. But yeah, you're just so manly. I'm sure Brittany'll *love* you."

"That's the goal. I'm hoping I can go back to her place. Apparently she lives near here."

"She does look familiar. I probably have served her, but who the hell even knows."

"You dare me to chug this one? It's like pretty full."

Nat smiles and rolls her eyes. "Sure, boy."

You throw your PBR back and chug chug chug away, all the way down until it's empty. You slam down the can, crush it with your hand, and sigh, "*Ahhhhh!* Hits the spot. What do I owe ya?"

"It's 15 bucks."

"What?"

"Yeah. 5 bucks per can of beer."

"You gotta be shittin' me. No way a PBR is worth *that*. All this shit is like cheap as hell."

"I mean, sir . . ."—saying "sir" now, you think, and treating you like just another piece of shit who walks through her door every single day—". . . that's the price."

You say, "Well, I hope I can get my pizza for free." You put down a twenty. "See ya, Natalie."

"See ya, Stevie."

"I hate Stevie."

"Well, I hate Natalie—so we're even."

You grin. "Touché. I'll catch you later."

Nat nods. "Yup. Bye, asshole."

four

Looking around the outside of the bar, you know you have to walk a very tiny bit to Downtown Pizza, but you know there's only, like, maybe 15-minutes left until your scheduled meet with Brittany—but you know damn good and well she will be fashionably late—so you have your hands in your pockets, walk left, and head toward the pizza place, a thought of wonder in your "man-ish" eye.

You think for a moment of last year, the time when you went to Thailand for a week, and how you were on Tinder, looking around for some quality Thai pussy. You were told by countless friends that there were 5-dollar prostitutes; but that seemed lazy, arbitrary, and frankly boring to you; you wanted a challenge, a hunt for a woman who vaguely doesn't want you, but you somehow, someway coerce her into sleeping with you. Even bigger points if she's married, you believed.

You think about how you got off the plane and didn't even get a driver to take you to some swanky hotel on the outskirts of Bangkok. You simply walked and had let your mind wander —just like you are now, except with a phone in your right hand, and your thumb consistently swiping right on every Thai girl that was in the area. You saw the people staring; you saw countless women, some giggled, some stared. You had a fairly big amount of cash in your pocket, and about 3,000 USD on your debit card. You were going to be a king for that week.

And then the matches started rolling in as you walked. You were looking at women—all types of women; mostly petite, Thai (obviously), and absolutely fuck-able. You looked at them and thought of something to say, a pickup line, a sign of some sorts that makes you vaguely look like a dickhead . . . but a "playful" dickhead at that, the kind of techniques that made you score with plentiful amounts of American girls in your local area, the pointless compliments not catered towards their looks but of something they chose, like their shirts they wear in photographs, earrings, makeup, *any*thing that requires some effort besides just being born with huge tits and a fat ass.

As you were thinking of sending a message, you received a few from these Thai broads that were claiming you were "cute." You think about their pussies and how wet they would all get because, culturally, you have heard that men in Thailand generally look for marriage and not flings, but the women that are hot have a shortage of men specifically out to fuck them—but obviously the broads want nothing to do with prostitution, so they use dating sites like Tinder or the like. . . . You grinned and laughed while walking toward a local soup kitchen with a sign that showed unbelievably low prices, and for premium rice noodles. You headed inside and made a response to this broad on Tinder who you couldn't even pronounce the name of:

You: Hi, I'm in town for a week and I'm looking to meet some cool Thai chicks. Are you one of them? Because if not I'm gonna have to un-match you, and that would be unfortunate, being as you are possibly one of the cutest little things I ever did see before my very eyes.

You read the message over and kind of rolled your eyes because those kinds of messages would have never worked toward hot, white-privileged American women who get literally hundreds of messages from guys: good, decent, desperate, and handsome to the hot chick's personal tastes. You thought about these Thai women, and how all those Thai men having incredibly small cocks, no sense of talking to them, no sense that they actually are horny creatures wanting cock, and how you're the one and only white boy, clearly American, who is providing the servitude of dick for them to happily take. You sent the message and waited.

You went into the soup kitchen and ordered plain rice noodles with some pork swimming around in the bowl. You paid the man, tipping him 200% what the food had actually cost, and his eyes widened and he made weird noises of surprise and, you assume, thank-yous. You nodded, grabbed your bowl, sat and ate. It tasted good. It tasted better than the crap in America that is not real and is about ten times more in price. You thought of the chefs there taking you for granted like all the other American customers that walk into their restaurants. You thought all of this as you swallowed down your lovely soup.

Your phone beeped that obvious Tinder notification tone, and you opened the app and read from the Thai girl who you couldn't even pronounce the name of. She wrote:

(unpronounceable):   You so cute American! I don't speak good English too good. Where R you? Its late. We should of go to a club and dance!

You vaguely were surprised it was that easy. You sent her your number. Immediately she texted you. After careful—and effortless—conversation, she told you the address to the club she spoke of. You got it, threw it into your Google search application, and noticed it was about a mile away. You started walking.

Everything around you was busy, smokey, with life, pursuit, and hustle. Everyone was working but everyone was happy, too. It's was a privilege to work; it was survival of the fittest. You don't deserve, you earn. You smiled at that sight. For that whole mile walk, you said "hi" to every Thai woman that passed by you, even if they had a man—husband, father, brother, attorney, paster, whatever—beside them, and literally every single one smiled at you. One even stopped and you had a mild conversation with her about a food place around the corner that "you American should definitely try," she suggested. You hugged her and went back to the task at hand: walking.

There was a line at the club. Everyone looked nothing like the flashy, superficial way you're used to from the club scenes in America; everyone was dress comfortably, in whatever they wanted, and nobody cared. You pulled out your phone and called the Thai bitch. She answered: "Hey! Where you are?!" It's noisy on her end of the line. You said, "Um, yeah, I'm outside. Are you inside?" "Yes! I come out!" The phone hung up, you were looking around and were thinking how odd this was, you being in a foreign country, alone, on a whim, and how absolutely crazy this all was. The fact that every American thinks of any country as third-world and refuses to go, but is deprived of some of the greatest experiences they will ever see, like Thai pussy, Thai noodles, Thai noodle suggestions, and Thai lines that you don't even have to go in, purely because you're American, white, people think you're rich, and a cute Thai bitch comes running out, grabbing your arm, saying (and wrongfully pronouncing), "Steven!"

You were pulled inside. There was a guy in front, much like a bouncer, but he didn't really seem to care, nor did he appear to let people in. You passed him. The inside was unbelievable. Smokescreen, lights flashing, weird, exotic hip-hop beats playing . . . It was a jungle inside there—of *drunken Thai fucks,* you thought. You got on the dance floor, no time to scope for more prospects. The Thai girl was all over you. You asked, loudly to be heard, "Were you, like, *here* already? On Tinder?" She said, "Yas! I *is!* It was getting boring!" You looked around and everyone appeared to be dancing very stiffly, as if the song warranted a specific dance. You said to the Thai bitch, "Let's dance." You spun her around, her back and ass up against you, her little, tiny (but somehow plump) Thai ass, and you moved her hips around. She was giggling. You giggled too, hoping she had never danced like this. She turned around abruptly and said, "I'm dancing like slut! Do you not like?"

You shook your head, spun her back round, and basically had thrusted your hips into her ass. Other Thai women flocked towards you. Then another, then another. Eventually, an entire group of Thai chicks was all over you, and your mind was blown. You had put your arm around two of them and started making-out with them both, taking turns as you did. You looked around and you were thinking for a moment that God exists, that he's up there, deep in the Netherlands of space, watching you and giving you this gift of sluts, and saying, "Hey buddy! *Yo!* You get those sluts!" But then you quickly shook that off and realized that God can never, ever grant you gifts such as that, only The Dark Lord, Satan, most awesome-est being ever (though you don't believe in *him* either), could ever make this happen—but even then both are entirely fictional. This world isn't all black & white, you think.

"Let's go back to your place, cutie," one of the sluts in your right arm squealed. "Yeah!" the other in your left agreed. So you said, "I kind of just got off the airplane. I'll call us a ride."

You walked them out of the club and out into the night, in the grimy, wet streets, and pulled out your phone, opening up your Uber application, and you were hoping that Uber even existed in Thailand. It did. 5-minutes later, a car arrived. The women giggled and said, in unison, "You so sexy!" You got inside the ride. You told the driver to take you to the closest hotel, something nice, something fancy. "Marriott Hotels, sir?" he asked. You nodded. "Yeah, buddy," and you all started to drive. The entire time you were making-out with one chick and were fingering the other's pussy from under her skirt. She wasn't wearing panties. You were excited. Eventually, the car stopped . . . but you kind of didn't want it to; you wanted the world to always be an Uber drive with two Thai sluts in the back.

The guy got paid via debit card (and you didn't tip him a single dime) and you had your arm around the two Thai sluts coming out of the car. There was some kind of streetlight above you three. You got to see their faces and you realized they weren't the chick you met up with on Tinder initially. You thought for a moment what she was doing at that moment, if she was bummed-out that she didn't score some white cock, that she wasn't getting laid by a "rich" American boy; and then you thought this is probably what it feels like being those hot chicks you would try to fuck in America and got rejected by in your earlier twenties, and you think of this power and how, yes, of course anyone would abuse this, just in the same way those hot American chicks did: you have a plethora of potential partners, so you pick the ones you deem "most worthy."

You were heading inside the hotel, nobody was in the waiting room, as if nobody had the funds necessary or the care to, you probably thought. Still with the Thai sluts in both your arms, you got to the help desk. "Hey, one room, one bed, whatever." "No problem, sir!" The guy's eyes were squinty, very oriental, and you wondered if he could even see the screen he was looking at. He said, "Yup, got one for top floor." "Penthouse?!" "No, sir. Next to penthou'." "Cool." Makes no sense, but whatever, right? You handed him a couple twenties and said, "Keep the change. For you." He went wide-eyed. You obviously paid too much, but whatever, if it got the Thai sluts pussies wet, the money was worth spending. So the guy handed you your room keys, you walked to the main lobby, got into the elevator, the two Thai sluts making-out with each other while you watched creepily, grinning the entire time, and you finally get to your floor.

You walked out; the sluts followed. You found your room. You couldn't remember the name of it, but you made a guess that it didn't matter. You walked in, it was a shit place, smelled like a weird mixture of dog and piss, specifically from a human, with high amounts of ammonia or some other shit you couldn't even put your finger on—you're not a scientist. You looked toward the bed, then the sluts, then the bed, and you said, "Strip." They nodded, giggled, and held hands together, prancing and seemingly happy. They undressed. You stopped them. "Slower," you ordered. "Slow, slow, slow . . . I want to see you both bend over while you take those panties off." They said, "Oh silly, we don't wear panties!" "Even better," you grinned. "Strip slowly." "Yas," one of them said. And you watched them take their clothes off. Nothing matters of the material. You thought of all the girlfriends you had that spent time buying lingerie that always seemed to be two sizes too small, and how pointless it seemed to you, the fact that it always came off the second you saw them with it on. (Though you don't know why you had thought this, considering no lingerie was present.)

The sluts were naked. "Get on the bed," you ordered. They

did; they climbed in. You started unbuttoning your collared shirt. One at a time they went, the girls giggled. The shirt came off. You vaguely have what is called a "dad bod," which most American women prefer nowadays because of the idea of a muscular guy being not a "real man," and how most women want you to be having "a little something extra," but not *too* much. This is what you were told anyway by a hot chick on your Facebook account once. You said to the Thai sluts, when you sat down on the edge of the bed, "Slap my back." They said, "Huh?" You said, "Shut the fuck up and do it, bitches." You didn't even look over to them. They started giving you love taps. You laughed, "What the fuck, yo? Harder! *The fuck* you think this is?!" They slapped harder, and harder, and harder, and finally, you said, "Stop."

You stood. Down your pants went. Your cock was ready, already hard. You faced the sluts. You said, "Both of you lay on the edge of the bed. I want to see your holes." They looked at each other and had this strange look on their faces. They complied, though, and gave you what you wanted. You looked at them, those quality vulvas. One had clearly seen better days, the other, well, the other looked average—not the best but not the worst. "This'll do," you said as an after-thought, and you started fingering them both. They started to moan. You fingered harder, so hard in fact that it almost felt like you were pulling on a rotisserie chicken's ass, the bone right there, tugging backward on your middle and ring fingers. The sluts moaned more. Your cock was so hard it actually hurt, actually felt like it may have had too much blood in it. You said, "Ready?" The girls said nothing, so that's always permission . . . obviously. You went for the one with the beat-up pussy, because it's always good to get the aggression out on the pussy that has run through a few cocks.

You jack-hammered it, feeling almost no friction, no tightness to her at all. It always felt as if you're lightly touching your cock and vaguely jacking off. So you just fucked her like crazy, warming up. You got bored. Both the sluts were moaning like crazy. One was sucking the one's left tit, the one you were inside. Side-stepping, you switched to the other pussy. Even worse. She wasn't wet enough. It felt like sandpaper was pulling on your cock and you could barely push yourself in and out of her. You looked down, spit, wasn't budging. You slapped your hand on the other vag, gaining the juices from *it*, and you lathered around your cock. You inserted again. Much better. You went slow, then hard, then fast. Pretty soon seconds turned to minutes turned to, well, about 20-minutes . . . You were not that into it. In fact, you just stayed on that one pussy. You were about to cum. You said, "Both of you, face me on the edge of the bed." They did without question. Their faces were sweaty, almost animal-like. You squirted your load on both their faces, one of them only had a few drops, the other took most of the hit. You looked up at the ceiling, standing there, thinking, *How can I possibly get rid of these whores?*

You bent down and grabbed your wallet from your back pocket. You handed the sluts a twenty and said, "That's for you both. Don't spend it all in one place. I gotta get to sleep now. It was nice having you two here, for, you know, what it's worth." They both looked at you like you were nuts. One of them said, "We aren't sex-ladies, okay?" The other one, well, the other one said, "Then *I'll* take money, more for me!" You didn't listen to the remainder of the conversation. You walked over, still naked, to their clothes at the end of the bed. You grabbed them, bunched them up, and said, "Here, get out." They stood, wiped off their faces with their hands, and grabbed the clothes. They stormed out the door, no goodbyes said. You turned the corner and were heading to the bathroom to take a piss.

While pissing, you looked up at yourself in the mirror. You wanted to talk to yourself, but it was no use. You see, you wanted to say so badly that you could have treated those sluts better, you could have shown them a good time, you could have not been a dickhead. But then you knew that you probably wouldn't have gotten off. You never do, especially for women you don't "love." It was odd you even came at all. You were thinking, while the last drops come out of you, *The more attractive and aesthetically pleasing a woman is, the less I want to get to know her on a personal level, and the more I want to procreate with her with the intent on having children with the highest survival traits.* This is nothing new. You went to bed and slept peacefully, dreaming about lions.

And this Thailand vacation went all through your head while you are sitting down at Downtown Pizza, waiting for Brittany Tinder. Your phone vibrates in your pocket. You grab it, it's a text. It's from Brittany asking where you're at. "Outside," you reply back. A few moments later, you feel a hand on your shoulder. You turn around and it's the cutest, most stunning black chick ever. Plump ass, crazy long hair, little waist, prettiest face, and she's smiling. She says, "Hey, Steven. So let's eat, huh?" You stand and say, "Sure." She grabs your hand and leads you inside Downtown Pizza. That smile of hers burns in your mind for an odd amount of time. You think about all the smiles that have faded away the more chicks got to know you and the more they realized how shitty of a man you really are. You think about that smile fading from Brittany at the end of this date, when you're obviously and inevitably buried deep inside her warm, fat, juicy vajayjay. You look up and hear, "Are you ready to order, sir?"

five

"YEAH, I'LL JUST HAVE a slice of pep."

You look over at Brittany saying this, she is looking at this guy behind the counter helping you both and she says to him, "Yeah, just pepperoni and cheese. And can I get those little red things you sprinkle on top?"

"Peppers?" the guy says.

"Yeah. That. *Thanks!*"

You're thinking, *This girl literally doesn't know what peppers are called. This should be* very *interesting.*

You and she sit and wait until she starts talking.

"So, Steve, how are ya?"

"I'm okay, I guess. Just thinking about past stuff."

"Like what?"

"Thailand."

"You visited Thailand! That's awesome! What did you see there?"

"A lot of desperate people."

"Yea', it's unfortunate. 3rd-world countries are a problem."

"Yeah. 3rd-world is right." You roll your eyes.

"Where else have you traveled to, Steve?"

"I don't know. Thailand was the only place that interested me."

"Why?"

"The, uh . . . people. I love how . . . *open* they are."

"Oh, that's cool." She laughs. "Are you liberal?"

You want to tell her the stereotypes of all liberals, how they like new behaviors, new things, new equalities that are completely petty and arbitrary, that you're a militant, atheistic conservative–republican. You want to refrain from saying this because you don't want to upset her, you don't want to lose a chance of getting some. But then you think of her being a Christian and—

"Wait," you say, "nobody ever asks about politics or religion on first dates."

Brittany laughs. "I know. I'm just screwin' with you."

"Are *you* a liberal?"

"Eh, not entirely. I have Christian values."

"Do you lean more left or right?"

"More left, in a lot of ways."

You could have spotted that a mile away. You should have hated on liberals like you always do on the internet, trolling everybody, having the sick satisfaction of ruining peoples' beliefs, of making them think in a new way—that is true progress, true revolution. You say to Brittany, "Me too."

She asks, "Are you a Christian?"

And just then, the guy behind the counter says, "Order up, you two!"

Brittany grins. "Let's eat outside, Stevie."

You both grab your pizza slices, and she gets handed the pepper shaker from the guy behind the counter; she says "thanks" graciously, nonchalantly, as if it's expected. You and her head outside and sit at the table closest to the door, right to your left when you first walk out. The table is dirty; it has little crumbs and bits of water droplets on it. You take a napkin given to you from your pizza-guy whatever-thingy and wipe it all off. Brittany stares. You guys take your first bites. Brittany asks you the question again:

"So, are you a Christian?"

"I already told you on Tinder."

"Yeah, but I want to be sure—it's important to me."

That's a given. If you have any hope of fuckin' this chick, you better say what she wants; so you say, specifically, "Yes, I'm an evangelical Christian."

She says, "Oh, thank God! What church do you go to?"

You're stumped. You haven't stepped foot inside a church probably since elementary school, a time when you were an innocent creationist, hoping that some God, some creator, made you and loved you, until you read that he had killed tens of millions of people just for disagreeing with him in a little book called *The Holy Bible*. You answer, "I just worship at home —I kind of just like my privacy."

Brittany says, "I respect that. Rogue. Mysterious. I like it." She smiles. "I go to the one south of P—— and F————."

"Really? That's wild. Me and my friends use to skate there."

"Skate? Like roller-blades?"

"No, skateboards. Like four wheels. It's a long story. I wrote a book about it. Just for fun."

"You wrote a book? Oh yeah, that's right. You told me."

"A few. That one didn't do well. But I didn't care, it was more for me than for my readership. I just wanted to make a memory book."

"That's awesome!" Brittany takes a bite of her pizza. "Eat, Steven. Food is gettin' cold."

You have been taking bites this whole time; *she* is the one who hasn't been. You flirtatiously say, "Speak for yourself, baby —I'm chowin' down, and you're the one gettin' cold food."

She grins. "You're so cute. I like when guys call me out on my shit. It's hot." You envision her saying the word "hot" spelled as *hawt.*

You can't help it, you ask, "You like hawt guys, huh?"

She nods. "Oh yes, very much so. Do you?"

"Guys?"

"No, silly! I mean girls! Like girly-girls."

"Duh! I'm with *you,* right? If I wasn't here, I would be out somewhere else, chasing tail. Probably the beach somewhere."

She goes silent. *Oh shit,* you're thinking, *did I say the wrong thing?*

She finally says, "We should go to the beach. It's a nice day."

You look up and down at her: "Uh, do we have the right clothes on?"

She says, "So *what?* Let's just take our shoes off and watch the water. Sounds fun."

You're not the type that is romantic, obviously—or even remotely into doing anything other than sex with a hardbody. You want to tell her that it's waste of time, that you typically watch the beach alone, in peace, without anyone around. You typically do it not to look at the beauty but to look at the world as a big, blue dome. You go to the beach to see the brightness and to look up at the sky and realize how small you are, how far up the sky is. You're in a bubble. You're in a bubble both literally and personally. You want nobody in your bubble. If you could, you would just lay down at the beach and do nothing. You have thought about being a beach bum. A bum without a woman, alone. You know that Brittany *is* the romantic type. It's possible just because of the suggestion of the beach. Or maybe it's just innocent fun. Who knows? The point is that if you want sex you will say the following:

"Yeah, sure. Let's go. Can we walk?"

And she laughs. "Oh, Steve! You're such a sap! I'm not going to the beach with a Tinder guy I just met. You *nuts?*"

"Yeah," you sigh, relieved, "I *am* nuts. Sorry. But hey, I have nuts, that's why I'm nuts."

Brittany says, "You're so peculiar. . . ."

For a couple of seconds, you both say nothing, munching on your pizzas. You think, for this small expanse of time, what is going through her mind: Is she thinking about the quality of the cheese, bread, and pepperoni? and how it correlates to her value of this date? Or how about what you think of her clothes, or if she's attractive? Is she thinking about if she made a mistake coming here? These are the questions you ask yourself, and strangely, they are the same questions that keep you busy with women, the same questions that make you steadily continue to hunt for them. Gaining attention from women is a thirst that never goes away. To you it's a deep, boiling shot of drugs injected into your mind/psyche. You're like a junkie, mindlessly chatting with any woman, or mindlessly swiping right on all women, just for them to give you a smidge of attention.

"What are you thinking about?" Brittany asks. "Your mouth is wide open. Eat your pizza."

Your mouth is in fact wide open, but it doesn't matter to you; you shake your head and say, "Sorry about that. Just daydreaming."

"It's okay. When did you join Tinder?"

"Couple weeks ago." This is a lie; you actually joined pretty much the day it was released on the app store. You loved the idea of only being linked-up with people that share your same physical attraction; it makes life so much faster, easier, and better when it comes to dating, flirting, et cetera. You say to

Brittany, "I'm actually not into the app at all. I was thinking about deleting it."

"Yeah, me too. It's boring sometimes. All the guys do on there is say how hot I am and very vulgar things."

"They're amateur. That's not how you get anywhere with quality women."

"Right! Thank you! *Knew* I made the right choice by coming here." She smiles. "What was your longest relationship? If you don't mind my asking."

"Not at all. 5 months."

Brittany squints. "Just 5 months!?"

"Yeah, I know," you laugh passively, "it's a long story that I'm actually thinking about writing soon. Just hard to entertain women for long enough. They always want more out of me. They always want to take things from me to make their lives better."

"I hate that."

"It's a pain, but I'm glad to be single now."

"Good. It's always good just to find yourself. I dig it." She drops her crust on her plate. "I'm done," she says. "Finish up. I want to check out the library that's near here. I always go."

"Yeah?" you say, taking a few more bites. "Uh, yeah, you read often?"

"Sometimes." She shrugs. "Hopefully we'll find one of your best-sellers in there." She grins. "Just joking."

"*Ha!*" you fake-laugh. "Funny. All you'll find is book-shits by that shit author, James Patterson. He sucks a fat one. I hate that guy. How arrogant do you have to be to make 'book shots'? 'Read in under two hours!' Gimme a break, fag."

Brittany laughs. "I know what you're talking about. That's funny. I've seen those displays at bookstores. You know James lives like a couple miles from here, right?"

"I'm aware. He sucks ass, the ghost-writer-hiring son-of-a-bitch."

"Someone's jealous."

"Yeah." You take the last bite of your pizza, wipe your hands with Brittany's napkin she didn't use, and say, "Let's do the library thing."

"Okay."

You stand up, walk inside Downtown Pizza and pay for your two slices. Nat's free pizza request was a lie; the guy didn't know who you were talking about. You walk back out, hold out your hand, and Brittany takes it.

You both walk not even a few steps and eventually get to the library of downtown Lake Worth. You climb up the steps, being sure Brittany is in front of you in case if she falls or something. You open the door for her, she says "thanks" and you both walk inside.

The place smells of old books. "Love this smell," you comment passively.

"I know," Brittany says. "We gotta check out the fiction side."

"What fiction do you like?"

"I like Christian fiction, honestly."

The thought comes to mind that it pains you to have to lie about your religious views, but these are the things you do for women. It's not even the sex that is of actual value to you, it's the gatekeepers you have to persuade: the women themselves. They're the ones you have to sway. They're the ones that make it worth it. By lying effectively, you have won the game of chess. These are thoughts that go through your head, and so you accept it and continue on.

At the Christian fiction section, you watch Brittany's eyes narrow and appear to seek for a title in particular. "I can never find it in this library, and I know they have it."

You ask, "What is it?"

"It's a book called *The Shack*. Have you read it?"

You haven't. "Yes, I have," you lie anyway. "Great book. About a guy in a shack finding God."

She looks up at you and smiles. "Indeed! I *love* that book!"

You totally guessed correctly based on context clues. You quickly divert her attention elsewhere.

"Hey, uh, do you like science at all?"

"I do! What do you like to read about?"

"I like Biology."

"I like the space stuff. Anything physics or deep space is so interesting!"

"I hate space so much," you say.

"Why?"

"It scares me." You scratch your head. "I don't know why. I think it's because I don't understand it at all. Like I don't understand the whole deep space thing and how vast it is; it just belittles me."

Brittany hugs you and says, "God loves us and is gonna show us the way, darling."

You remember that you're playing a role of a creationist. You realize anything science will not correlate. You divert her attention again.

"Do you like art?"

"Oh yeah, I love it! I used to draw a lot."

"What of?"

"Mostly portraits and stuff."

"I drew cartoons when I was a kid. Mostly aliens and comics."

"I try to recreate big historical paintings."

You can tell this will, yet again, lead to creationist jargon that you don't want to entertain. You divert again.

"That's, um, cool—where's your house?"

"My what?"

"Your house."

"Oh, I didn't hear you. I'm down the street."

"Can we chill there? Am I worthy enough to know where you live?"

Brittany smiles. "You're sweet. Sure. Want to go now?"

You say, "I mean, we just got here. We can if you want."

"I can tell you don't like conversation in a library."

"Yeah, it just stresses me out. I don't want to appear dumb."

"It's fine." Brittany grabs your hand. "Let's walk."

You both exit the library and stroll down the sidewalk, southbound.

six

INSIDE YOUR RIGHT FRONT POCKET, there's this vibration from your phone that you vaguely don't want to pick up. You hope the person calling or texting will give-up after a few more tries, or better yet, just lose your number entirely. But you have the sneaky suspicion that that is not going to pan out in that way, even as you mute the phone's vibration and simultaneously grab Brittany's hand, hoping that her house is as close by as possible.

"How far are you?" you ask her.

"Not *insane* far. Why?"

"Just wondering. I hate walking."

"Yeah . . . Sure . . . *Someone's* an eager beaver," and her saying this phrase vaguely gives you an odd sense of déjà vu.

You both eventually reach Lake Avenue and North Federal Highway, still heading southbound. Always you thought of this area being a bit ghetto, a bit too "cultural," as politically correct as you can be, and you never even had the thought in your mind to head down this way. You always stay downtown, always on Lake. And if you do find yourself heading eastbound you always end up at the park, the bridge, or the beach, where you have taken dozens of dates to in the past. Why, you remember a time when you took a mother down there at midnight and she took off her shirt, wearing only her bra, and it was the first time you two met on Tinder. You both took your shirts off with the intent of laying on them and looking up at the night sky.

This mother chick said to you, pointing, "You see that one. Right there in the middle."

"Yeah."

"That's Mercury."

"You're full of shit."

"No, I'm serious."

"Whatever," it was no use in correcting her (and later on in the night you did research and found out that this mother was, in fact, correct).

She said, "Steven, what do you think about?"

You never were really asked this by a Tinder date, or really any female for that matter. The question surprised you, and at first, you didn't have a clear answer, you just thought for about ten seconds and heard another "Steven . . . ?" before you said:

"Sometimes I think about how small and insignificant I am, being here on planet Earth. I think about the billions of people here—moms, dads, pets, brothers, sisters, your kids" (the mother laughed) ". . . or whatever else is living on here—and I think about their lives and how they, too, are also equally as small as me. I think about how every animal on this planet is selfish and only does things for their specific needs. They just want to survive, live, indulge in anything they can get their hands or paws on that gives them a sense of pleasure . . .

"I think about this sometimes and I cry because, well, where does that leave me, this human named Steve, huh? Where am I? What am *I* doing here? I used to think if I was a good person, or if I had always done my best and helped people out, that one day I would be paid back. But even asking that question is selfish because I'm hoping to be 'paid back,' even before doing any good deed. It was then that I knew that I was just as shitty as every serial killer, rich Wall Street coke-head, or dog on this planet: I was simply here to live and indulge and gain pleasure. And I think about every single time I ever made a choice in my life and how it relates to me. I think about every person I've ever done something for and how I only wanted to help someone or give them something just because it satisfied *me*, or gave *me* some shred of pleasure, to see them experience joy; it was like a sick, twisted exchange of feel-good chemicals in the brain: dopamine, oxytocin, serotonin, maybe adrenaline, et cetera . . .

"I think about this and I always wondered where I fit into the equation, but even then it's I, I, I, and never anyone else. I'm just selfish. It was then that I realized it, and it was then that I realized that I realized it and nobody else did. Nobody else really knows the amount of selfishness they have in their lives. So I began reading; I began reading everything there was to consume on science, politics, space, sci-fi, you name it. I read everything that brought misery or indulgence or doubt on the planet—misogyny, atheism, sex, alcohol, comedy, biology, taboo subjects, controversial subjects—and it was the only way my need for happiness could be fed.

"In the pit of my stomach I always knew I was empty inside, and I always knew that that emptiness could never be filled with money or clothes or houses or marriage or anything else trivial that society aims for. I always felt that none of it was real or that it was pointless. Nothing that people told me was the truth, even in the books I read. Everything was discovery, opinion, and based on belief—nothing was known for sure. Nothing was always nothing. Even before I was born I felt nothing. And it has led me to believe that upon my death I will feel the fleeting feeling of nothingness and absence, just like I did before my birth. I thought of the validity of life and how pointless it was, and I slipped into nihilism. Blissful indulgence, graceful, shameless nihilism.

"Through all of this, I numbed myself. I had no more depression, no more anxiety. Nothing bothered me anymore. I felt no pain, anger, jealousy, sadness, happiness, or any feeling anymore. My goal was to not even be a living thing or even be a living human anymore. My life's goal from then on was simply to observe, that's all. And I guess that's why I wrote, that's why I am always creating and writing because it makes me feel better to feel like I could create something from nothing. And though I am and always have been an atheist at heart, I have always liked the idea of being a god that could create something from nothing, as ironic of a god as that sounds . . .

"But I digress. The point I'm getting at is I read books and it enabled me to both simultaneously learn and to not give a shit about anything or anybody. Eventually, when we do die, we will be forgotten. Everyone who knows us, when they die, your memory inside their minds will die with them. Everything expires and everything doesn't last the test of time. Time is an illusion but time is everything. Time is what ultimately is the true beginning and end. It is the creator of everything. Time is everywhere and nowhere. Time is God. Time is both proven and disproven, seen and unseen. Everything is at the mercy of time. Everything cannot last. Therefore, every living thing on this planet—*heck!* even the things that are inanimate—are going to become nothing and forgotten and pretty much nonexistent. No lives matter. Not a single thing matters. The only things that may matter are my addictions that I have. That's about it. It's all pretty much anyone cares about.

"The sun and moon and stars eventually die. Everything begins and ends. The planet Earth I dwell on will end and nothing ever stays the same or even matters even the slightest bit. I look at the world around me and it's hard to even want or begin to care. I look at these stars in front of me and see how vast they are and how small I am and how small they are compared to time. I don't know. Maybe I'm crazy. Maybe I'm depressed. These are all pointless emotions. Everyone looks at me and says, 'You're so negative all the time. Why can't you be happy? Why can't you see the world and see it as beautiful?' And you know what, I do. I agree! But what does my opinion matter? I'm not entitled to anything. Life is here, life is not here.

"Why do we even ask questions? Why do we even try or care or do anything with this little time we have? It's a very odd thing to live, isn't it, Jennifer?" (The mother that was beside you's name was Jennifer.) "And even see any of this as a gift. You can sit here and be optimistic, pessimistic, good or bad. You can sit and ponder, but honestly, none of this matters in the grand scheme of things. You can choose to view any of this as bad or good, but I really don't give a shit. Again, no lives matter. Is that good or bad? I prefer to live the life of "I don't know," the true answer to everything we have ever known, will know or could know. It's just whatever.

"I devote my life to observing. In the meantime, I will be here doing it from moment to moment. In the meantime, I will devote my life to selfishness. My altruism will be masked by selfishness. The people I love are so wonderful and beautiful. I love them but I know love is a production of oxytocin. I will from moment to moment do whatever feels right: fuck chicks, drink beer, sing songs, write, dance, talk, cry, look and see, drink and eat, sleep, do cartwheels, pet my dog, run, walk, jump, breathe, and just simply *be*. . . . I'll embrace bad and good feelings and just *be*. That's my philosophy. I may not think of myself as human or living, but I am simply being. That's what I think about. Hope you understand, Jennifer."

And that mother that day, just you and her, lying on the beach, shirts off, looking up at the stars, on you think maybe a midnight Friday—that mother turned to you and kissed you. She was crying while she did. She told you she never heard better words come from a person. So she took off her pants, panties, and kept her bra on. She unzipped you and grabbed your cock out. You were only half-hard. She inserted you inside herself and she rode you while seemingly having her head back. You wondered if while she was grinding you, looking up at the stars, if she felt a sense of beautiful nihilism that you have always felt. *But whatever,* you thought, per usual, shrugging mindlessly, *at least I'm getting some quality k-k-kitty! Yuck-yuck!*

And this is what you thought about while walking southbound down North Federal Highway with a gorgeous black woman named Brittany by your side. "We're here," she says, and she opens the door to her apartment, bottom floor (there are only two floors). You feel zoned-out but you smile because the wish was to get to her house as quickly as possible, and if daydreaming granted that, you think, then so be it.

You walk into her place. It smells odd—of cinnamon and a weird combination of candles you can't really put your finger on. You look around and see very minimal picture frames everywhere. This suggests that Brittany is an only child and doesn't have much family, or she is a millennial and doesn't like the idea of picture frames and carries all her photos in her handy-dandy smartphone to showcase to people she selectively wants to. You also look over and see her kitchen. It's plain. You bet she doesn't cook at all, or she does but it is very minimal and she claims to be a cook but isn't anything special—beans, rice, pizza, pasta, maybe the occasional chicken tenders. You don't even know anymore what people do or think, you can only just infer from the caves they have created. You have always thought that the inside of a house showcases exactly someone's personality. Your houses are messy in the places you don't dwell in, and clean and minimal in the places you do. Kitchen terrible, bedroom clean. You have always inferred that maybe this is how you treat people in some way: effort into the ones that matter, none in the ones that don't.

"Nice place," you tell Brittany. "Where's your television?"

"I don't, uh, have one."

"Why?"

"I don't watch TV. I have a phone and Netflix."

You realize this probably answers the picture frame question. You ask, "Do you have siblings?"

"That's kind of odd to ask—no, I don't. Only child."

"I see."

She goes silent for a moment and then says, "You hungry?"

You say, "We just ate pizza not too long ago."

"I know, but it was just one slice, you cheap bastard!" She winks. This is a flirty shit-test . . . obviously.

You smile and say, "You're so bad. I'll bet you're a good kisser."

She steps forward. "Am I?"

You think of all those times before you got laid and all the times males of all ages, sizes, and colors you've ever known that have told you to play it cool in these situations, "to be yourself," "to play your cards right." But frankly: it's better for you to take something and get a no than it is for you to not try and get a no. This was quickly how you realized women are. . . .

So you take a hold of Brittany and you start making-out with her. Your lips smack and you're tonguing all around the inside of her mouth. She's moaning while you're doing this and she vaguely is tonguing you back. "Hey—" you say, stopping. "Room."

She points behind her. "Over there."

You make-out with her again and walk forward, her walking backward, towards the bedroom. You think for a moment of the world pausing, and everything you do is simply for this moment: the blissful natural processes of sexual reproduction. You think of Charles Darwin and everything he stands for. You think in this moment how automatic everything feels. You touch whatever you want. They let it happen. You can be a man of status, and they let it happen. Grab them by the pussy. You can do anything. And oddly this gives you déjà vu again.

You and Brittany are in the room, still making-out. You pick her up, her legs wrapped around you. You fall forward— and I stress that you fall forward because she is the one you entirely hold—onto the bed. She says, "Damn. Fuck . . ." And you know exactly what she means: *You are a God and I want you.* Then she says, "Fuck me." You pull down your pants, she pulls down hers; you pull off your shirt, she pulls off hers. You don't even really look at each other; it's very selfish and you both appear to be in this for pleasure—or at least you hope that she's thinking it too. Gives a good excuse.

Naked. Condoms. Bed. Insert. Penis. Vagina. Moans. Groans. "Fuck me!" Says name. Says name again. Faster. Deeper. Slaps thigh. "Choke me!" You do what she says. You choke. "Harder!" You choke harder. "Harder, pussy!" You choke as hard as you can. It's not enough. "Pussy!" You think she's wild. You pin her legs back and jackhammer her. You think of her as a sex toy and this oddly makes you harder. "Fuck me! Fuck me, fuck me, Daddy!" You don't know why chicks always call you "Daddy." You blow a load. It's all inside the condom. You'd like to think of it as inside her, as filling her to the brim. Something about it makes you excited. You think it's some instinctual thing, a weird prehistoric, caveman-like need to make a female impregnated. Regardless, you're thankful we invented plastic around sexual organs to prevent this from happening and making an unfortunate, unwanted creature.

Thank nonexistent *God* for science and inventiveness!

"That was so great, Steven," your lovely whore comments.

seven

A CIGARETTE IS ALL YOU CAN THINK ABOUT as you lay beside Brittany, a black Tinder slut you've just fucked. You think about pulling one out at her place, in her bed, without her permission, and pulling out a Zippo lighter too, one that has a 1990s Jurassic Park emblem on it, and sparking it up. You want to see Brittany telling you that she doesn't approve, she wants to keep her place clean and smoke-free so she gets her security deposit back eventually when her lease expires. You think of all this and still want to inhale that fresh, sweet all-American Winston Reds cancer stick all the way down to the filter, and fling it onto her carpet after and go for round 2. But you don't have any, so the idea is just that: *an idea.*

"Damn, it's been awhile for me," Brittany says. "It's been, like, months."

"Yeah," you say. "It's been about maybe 2 hours for me."

"2 *hours?* What? How?!"

"I have a girlfriend. I fucked her before I went on this date."

Brittany goes silent. She turns to you. "Wait—you have a girlfriend?!"

The thought doesn't seem to come to her head that you had sex with another woman, just simply that you *have a girlfriend.* It's typical, you think; so you say, "Yes. I have a girlfriend who buys me Starbucks in the mornings and who I fuck like a whore and treat like shit."

Brittany's silent. Her eyes start to tear up. You think for a moment how terrible you are.

And then she bursts out a laugh with her head back.

"Uh . . ." you start, then stop. "Um, what . . . ?"

"Steven, you're so funny. You're messin' with me." Brittany cuddles with you, holding you close. She rests her head on your chest. "Tell me more about yourself."

You roll your eyes because this kind of thing always seems to happen to you when you are actually honest with people, especially women. You say, "I'm an awful human, a piece of shit scum of the earth. I go on Tinder specifically to hookup with chicks. I want to hopefully fuck at least a hundred chicks before I die. I've already surpassed that number and all it does is make me shoot for an even larger number. I'm terrible, don't you see?"

"You're not that terrible. I think you're a pretty cool guy."

"Why?"

"I don't know. Most guys that just want sex don't really go on actual dates, that's one. And two, libraries? Could've fooled me."

"Yeah, but I actually enjoy books. And *you* suggested that."

"That's another thing. You're smart *and* funny," she says, skimming passed your comment. "I do enjoy my time with you. I think you're a little too detached from me, but that's kind of why I like you. You're mysterious."

Mysterious. Hm, you've never been told that before, although you have made fun of the idea of a man being mysterious before around your group of friends, drunk around a campfire on a Saturday. But besides, "mysterious" is a flattering adjective. "Thanks," you say. "And you're, um . . ."

Brittany looks up. "Um?"

". . . Hawt."

She sighs. "That's, like, the worst. 'Hot' is so dirty. Like why not call me 'pretty' or 'cute' or 'stunning' or something else. That word is just too sexual for me."

"I mean, it's exactly what I meant then. Hawt. That's what you are."

"So you wanted to just fuck me?"

"Yes."

"Is that why you took me out?"

"Correct."

"You're such an ass." She smiles. "But whatever."

You say, "I'm also not a Christian."

She sits up and looks at you. "What?"

"Yeah," you shrug. "I don't believe in God."

"That's kind of fucked."

" 'Fucked?' Not very creationist of you to say, now is it?"

Her eyes narrow. "You really *are* an asshole."

You bat your eyes. "Now you know the real me, Ms. Sugar-tits."

She gives you a flirt punch, "Asshole!" and she smiles and cuddles with you some more.

After a beat, you say, "But seriously, I do actually have a girlfriend."

"I'm better than her."

"Probably. You guys both're wild."

"Am I freakier than she is?"

She isn't, but you lie and say, "Yeah."

"How so? Like what is it? Tell me."

"Uh, I don't know. You, uh— I don't know."

"*Nah!* Tell me!"

"Okay, okay. Well, it's kind of because you just give your

pussy to me. Like you have your legs open and it's just inviting. So I take it. I don't know."

Squint, neck moves back an inch or so, looking like you're a nut-job of some kind . . . "Your girlfriend doesn't do that?"

"Actually, she does . . ." you say. "I don't know. You both are good."

She changes the subject.

"Why don't you believe in God? I'm curious."

"Very hard to explain," you say. "Um, I guess I just simply don't like the idea of God. A guy creates me and then demands I worship him? and he created literally everything? including everything *bad*? It's just not cool to me. So I don't believe in it."

"So you do think there is God, you just choose not to?"

"No. I don't think there is. Yes, it would be arrogant to say God definitely does not exist because it's unprovable. But also God is an idea made up by human minds. Almost like a symbol of something. I just have no use for it. I just live my life."

"Yeah, but are you happy?"

"Not really."

"You would probably be happy with God. What does it hurt to believe?"

"Honestly, it's because I value truth more than anything else. That's all I want. Truth and reason. I want to know what is real and what isn't, what is proven and what isn't. I gravitate towards science because it works. Without it, we wouldn't have planes or doctors. It helps us and aids us. But besides science, I simply want the truth, even if I don't like the answer. I want to know where I stand."

"Yeah, but why not love God? He can help you."

"I've already tried to give religion a shot. It actually increased my sadness and dread. Every moment of every second I was worried if I was doing something wrong. I don't want to live my life like that. I refuse. I want to do things that *I* want to do."

"Yeah, but you could hurt yourself."

"Again, truth. That's all I want. True happiness, true joy. Truth."

"But you just said you're not happy."

"I don't think anyone is."

"I am. I know I am."

"Do you?"

"Absolutely!"

"I call bullshit. Most of what people teach us is to make some sort of fake happiness. They always, *always* say to 'fake it until you make it.' "

"Yeah, but it's true! You don't think so?"

You shake your head. "Nope. Not at all."

"You can't be *that* cynical."

"It's not even cynical or negative, it's life. If I'm not actually happy, I don't pretend to be. I don't even want to be around people who try to turn away from me just because I'm negative. All I want out of life is truth."

"Truth is what you make it."

"Wrong. Truth is entirely truth. Sometimes I lie, but it's for things most people don't lie about. Like I'll lie to purposely make myself look bad. One time I met this chick who asked what I did for a living. Guess what I told her."

"What?"

"A drug-dealer."

Brittany starts laughing. She says, "That's weird."

You say, "I know."

"What did she say?"

"Nothing really. She just kind of stopped talking to me."

"And you call that truth?"

"Yes. Reason being is because if you showcase to the world a frame of yourself that makes people think bad of you, you're going to filter out all the judgmental assholes who would have judged you regardless. That's another reason why I hate religion in general, and why it caused me so much pain. I hated the fact that it was the worst thing ever to be the worst thing ever."

"You're so weird, Steven."

"I know. I know I am. But I can't help it. The people who I connect with the best are always people with problems. My friend—one of my best friends—he was addicted to cocaine. I enabled him to do it. I partied with him, he would do lines at the bar. Key bumps. And he was the smartest man I knew. He had so much life to him. I hated how people thought of him as just a lowlife junkie. That's just the surface. And you know what? He stopped because of me. Obviously not entirely—he still does it from time to time—but still, he slowed *way* the hell down. And that's good enough for me. He knows everything about me, good and bad. People are so scared to know the bad that they just simply turn away."

"I see what you mean."

"I've literally fucked dozens of whores this month on Tinder, and you're added to the list. How does that make you feel?"

"Um, pretty shitty actually—I'm not a whore, Steven."

"I know you aren't. But I still say you are to insult you, to test you, to make you feel bad. How do I know you're a good friend or even a good lover if you can't even stick around for me during my bad?"

"Doesn't mean you should be an asshole."

"But in actuality, I'm not."

"I don't understand."

"Now you're asking real questions. What is the truth? What has this guy done? Has he lied? My past is only what I tell you. There is no proof. I very well could have been a 4.0 student at my high school, graduated from Harvard Law and passed the bar and became a lawyer for Dooie, Fuck'em, and Howe, and you wouldn't've even known it."

Brittany laughs and says, "You're just so . . ."

"So what?" you ask.

". . . Odd. But I like it."

"You like it?"

"Yeah." Brittany gives you a kiss. "I like it. I like you. We should hang more."

Oddly this doesn't feel like the right answer, you think. This feels strange. You were nothing but cruel to this girl, this nice, hot Christian girl with supposed morals and standards, and she is allowing you in.

"No," you say suddenly.

"No what?"

"I'm not interested in getting to know you."

"Why?"

"You're inconsistent."

"How?!"

You stand up, still naked, and say, "I'm getting out of here."

"Steven! Why?! Answer me!"

"You're a Christian girl, that means you want kids, right? And marriage, right?"

"Well, yes, maybe one day. What are you gettin' at?"

"That's what I thought. You have morals. You want things. I can't associate myself with a person who is on that level and doesn't judge me. It's sick."

"Steve, you're joking, right?"

You put on your pants.

"Steven?"

"What?"

"Are you joking?"

You put on your shirt and say, "No. I'm not."

"You're such a dick!" Brittany starts crying. "You claim to hate judgmental people, but look at you!"

You sit at the edge of her bed and put on your socks and shoes. Afterward, you say, "I gotta go."

"Where?!"

You think for a moment and smile, thinking of a movie you love. You say, "To go return some videotapes."

Brittany eyes you and says, unsure-like, "What the fuck . . . ?"

"Yeah."

"There isn't any more videotapes! The hell?"

"Oh yeah. Videotapes. Gotta return them."

"You're so full of shit. Leave!"

You stand up and grin; you say, "And this is my point. You didn't pass the test."

Brittany's startled. She doesn't say a word, she just stares at you. And you say, "Bye," and head out of her bedroom door and out the front door of her place. You hope you can find your way back to downtown Lake Worth, where your car is parallel-parked somewhere near some shitty dive bar.

eight

EVENTUALLY, WHEN YOU HEAD NORTH down Lake, you hit downtown Lake Worth, where you were just at not too long ago, where you fancied the finer things in life of fucking whores and drinking the blood of Christ. It is here in Lake Worth that you find your car, get inside, and note your fuel depletion.

"I'm on E," you sigh. You're always on E in life.

You start your car nonetheless and make way to the closest gas station, a Shell. It has dirt and shrubs on the walls on the side of the building, bottom to top. It could use a good, urgent pressure-cleaning, you think. There are expectantly two homeless, shoeless men sitting just outside the entrance of the gas station. You park beside a pump, turn off your car, step outside, and pull out your wallet. You slide your debit card into the card reader of the gas pump. Rejected. Go see the inside attendant. You sigh and start walking on inside. Before you go in through the doors, one of the bums asks, "Spare change, buddy? You got a dollar by chance?" and you ignore it and go inside anyway.

You walk up to the counter. "Yo," you say, getting the brown guy's attention. He seems to be stocking cigarettes. There doesn't appear to be anyone in the store.

"Yes, sir?" the brown guy says, standing up. "Ho' can I hel' you?" He's Indian.

You say, holding up cash, "Twenty on pump 2."

"Hokay, sir." The brown guy takes your money and you walk out.

You stand next to your car, pull out the pump. You start filling your tank and wait. You look towards the sky and see two, three birds, probably flying east somewhere, maybe to get food, maybe to get away from people (birds), or maybe just to simply fly and be what they are. You look back down and see one of the bums, a Caucasian male, walk up to you.

"Ay, man, you got a dolla'?" he asks.

"Nah. Sorry," you say, looking away.

"Come on, bro. I know you got somethin'."

"I don't got shit. Leave me alone."

"I saw you had money in your wallet."

"And?"

"And you should help a nigga out."

"But you're *white*," you inform him.

"And?" he says.

You shake your head. "Tell you what. I got 5 bucks."

"Yeah? Thanks, man. I'm just hungry as hell."

"But you gotta earn it."

This startles him. He says, "How . . . ?"

You grin and say, after a slight beat, "Kiss my shoes and bow down to me."

The guy's eyes go wide; he says, "The fuck?"

"You heard me. Get to kissin'." You pull out your wallet, pull out a "5" spot, and wave it around. "Kiss my shoe and get this money."

"You sick, bro," the bum says. "You sick as shit. How can you treat a man like that, bro?"

"How can you come up to a man asking for free money? Money that I worked hard for. Money that is mine and that you want to take with no return. Fuck that. What do *I* get out of it? Kiss my fucking shoes."

The bum seems to think for a moment. He looks behind him at his other bum friend or something. He turns around embarrassingly and gets on his knees in front of you. He leans forward. He looks up at you and says, "Come on, man. You can't be serious."

"Kiss it," you command. "Or no cash, Jack."

He leans forward and kisses your shoes, shoes that you have been walking in for months, shoes that you have walked through mud and dirt with your dog on Sundays at Okeeheelee Park, shoes that have stepped in gum, vomit (probably), pizza slices, rotten food, a dead bird, maybe dog crap, whatever. The bum kisses your shoes and then stands up abruptly. He says, "Okay, bro! Now gimme yo' cash!"

The gas nozzle clangs and stops, you take it out of your car and place it back into the pump holder. You look at the bum, grin, wad up the 5-dollar bill and throw it over him. It hits the ground, in a wet puddle. You say, "There's yo' shit."

The bum shakes his head. "Asshole. . . ."

While he walks toward the bill on the ground to go and pick it up, you simultaneously get into your car and start it up. You roll down the window.

"Hey!" the bum says, picking the bill up, shaking the water off of it. "This is a fuckin' *dollar*, yo!"

You shout, laughing while you do, "All you asked for, kid," and you press the gas and speed away going north down Lake, you assume. You don't even look behind you to see what the bum is doing, to see if he is jumping around, shaking his head, doing backflips because of how angry he is. Or maybe going inside and accepting his fate. Maybe buying a soda. Maybe realizing that he should get a job. Maybe realizing a lesson from this act you did. You think about all of this and finally, you come to the conclusion that he probably won't ever change his ways . . . And you won't either.

Still driving, you feel a vibration in your pocket from your phone. You pull it out. It's Janne. "Shit," you say, and pick it up. "Hello?" you say into the phone.

"Where the fuck have you been, asshole?! I've been trying to call you!" Janne says on the other end.

"Just driving around, gettin' food."

"I woke up to you not here, and I don't have a key and I didn't want to leave your house."

"So? You can. I'm near City Place. Nobody's gonna fuck with my apartment. I mean, friggin' Tamron is close by, but whatever—they don't bother shit."

"Not the point, Steven! I was literally at your house this entire time and I was too afraid to leave! I missed work because of *your* ass! Had to call in sick, which I never fucking do! *Ugh!* Get here, *now!*"

"Okay," you say and hang up. Probably not the best thing to do to an angry woman, you think; but you also think that she deserves it for being a royal pain in your ass. Immediately when you hang up, your phone starts blowing up, so you turn it off. You don't really have time for any such nonsense. You drive.

You drive and drive and you reach a point where you just watch the lines on the road zip on by, one by one, as if the present is in front of you and quickly behind you, as if both the future and past are never seen or have never been known to exist; it is only a reflection of one's desire to go from one place to another—and in your hellish case, a slut–whore at your residence. You finally make it to City Place nonetheless and park your car in the lot behind your place because you already know all the spaces are taken by your asshole neighbors and the lack of management creating enough spaces for said asshole neighbors. You park, get out, don't lock your doors (whatever), and walk towards your place. When you go through the gate leading to your courtyard full of your delicate neighbors, you see a little girl sitting at the table in the middle, reading a book.

You walk toward her and say, "Hey, you okay?"

She says, looking up, "Mhm! Just reading!"

"Good. What're you reading?"

"It's for my school. *James and the Giant Peach.*"

"Never read it. Always heard it's a good one." You sit beside her and ask, "Hey, so are your parents around?"

"Yes. I'm visiting my dad."

"Who?"

"I'm not allowed to say his first name. It's Steve."

"Oh. The second Steve above me. Yeah, he's a good guy."

Actually, he isn't. He once called a towing company to move your car one night when you took two spaces at once and were drunk. The tow truck took it off and you always had a hatred for Steve. Usually anyone named Steve is a scumbag, you think.

But anyways, the little girl says, "Yes he is!"

You say, "Where is he?"

"Inside. He just let me read a little while he watches television."

"Did he ever tell you not to talk to strangers?"

"Yes, but you seem nice. You don't look scary."

"The people who are less scary are the ones that are most scary. Always remember that."

"Really?"

"Oh yes." You nod. "Very much so. And they will hurt you if you're not too careful."

"Why are you here?"

"My girlfriend is inside my place right there." You point to it. "She's mad at me."

"Why?" The little girl blinks.

You say, "I don't really know. I'm kind of a bad guy."

"Are you a stranger to her?"

"Sure feels like it sometimes. I left her alone in my house and she had work, I guess. I went out to see another girl."

"That's sad. Why can't you just have one?"

"One girl?"

"Yeah! In church my pastor told me that's against one of the ten commandments. He said some word, I can't remember."

" 'Thou shalt not commit adultery'?"

"Yes!"

"Yeah. I do that all the time, and I'm not married."

"Aren't you gonna go to the bad place?"

"You mean Hell?"

"I'm not supposed to say it, but yes . . ."

"I don't really believe in it, but I'm sure I will if it's true. I doubt it, though."

"Why don't you like her?"

"My girlfriend?"

"Yes!"

"I do like her, but not in the same way she likes me. She likes me because I'm handsome and charming, I like her because she makes me feel good when we kiss and stuff."

"*Ew!* I'm not *supposed* to kiss!"

"You shouldn't. Save your kisses for the right kind of man. A non-stranger man."

"You seem nice, Mr. . . ."

"Steve. Just call me Steve."

"Daddy?"

You laugh at the irony. "Yes. Daddy. But I'm not your daddy. We just have the same name, that's all."

"That's pretty neat!" the little girl smiles.

"You're pretty cool yourself, little one."

"My name is Amber. I'm 8."

"Nice to meet you."

A beat happens between you two.

"Mr. Steve?"

"Yes, Amber?"

"What would it take to make you like her better?"

You think she is talking about Janne. "What would it take?" you ask, thinking about it for a brief moment. "I really don't know. I like girls that don't put up with my nonsense but also stick around. Call me out on my stuff but still love me. She doesn't do that at all. She just kind of goes with my antics. I'm not sure. She always never stays mad or sad or at all says what she thinks she's feeling. She just goes by whatever I tell her to go by. It's kind of depressing because most women are like this. Very hard to find one I'm looking for. One day I will, though."

"I like that," Amber says, "a lot."

"Yes. One day you'll find a guy to kiss and you'll be happy. But do me a favor, never, ever let him kiss others or make you feel a way that you don't actually feel. It's not good for you and you'll get hurt."

"Okay, Steven."

"My full name, huh? You're sweet."

Amber smiles. "Okay. I gotta get back to reading, now."

You say, "Good. I gotta go anyways. Be safe." You stand up,

lean forward, and kiss Amber on the forehead. You say, "Bye, 'Ber."

"My short name!" she says.

You just smile and shake your head. You walk away.

Opening the door to your apartment, you step inside and see the place is spotless. Entirely clean. You roll your eyes, close the door behind yourself. "Joanne!" you shout. "Where you at?" Your bedroom door opens. She comes storming out and cursing.

"Asshole! Why did you hang-up on me?!"

"My bad. Traffic."

"I don't give a shit if you crash!"

"Babe, stop. It's not that serious."

"I just can't believe how inconsiderate you are."

"But you love me, Sugar-butts."

"Stop!"

"What? No love?"

"I hate when you do this shit."

You step forward and give her a hug. You say to her, "I love you, Sugar-butts."

"Ugh." She looks up. You notice her eyes are glossy as if she has been crying, or as if she's touched. . . . Probably both. "I love you, too," she says.

"You can't be mad at me," you say and give her a kiss.

She stops you and smiles. "Still a total dick, though."

You feel a vibration in your pocket. You pull out your phone. It's a message from Brittany. It reads: "I'm sorry." You look at the time. It's about 3-ish o'clock. You say to Janne, "I think you'd better go. I don't want you to be cooped up in here any longer. Go to Sephora and get something nice." You pull out your wallet from your back pocket and hand her a hundred dollar bill. "Have fun, Sugar-butts. Love you." You smack her ass.

She smiles and says, "Dork!" and then walks out of your apartment.

It's quiet. So you do the one thing you love: you go to the bathroom, you shut the door, turn the light on, and sit on the toilet. You pull out your phone, set it on the ground, pull your pants down, and already you're hard as a rock. You grab your phone again and start-up PornHub. Mia Khalifa always is a good one. "Creampie" is even better. You spend a good 15-minutes looking for the perfect video. You find one and the chick on there says, "Fuck me, Daddy!" You blow your load into the toilet bowl water instantly. It floats there, dead-like, lost, confused, plasmic. You think about the virtually infinite number of children that never came to fruition just from you alone. You flush. You pull your pants up. You, you, you . . .

Reply to Brittany: "It's okay. I forgive you."

nine

Sparky seems to be lying down on the ground next to you as you sit on your couch, thinking of what to do with the rest of the day.

"Hey," he says, looking up at you, "scooch over."

So you scoot over. Sparky gets up on the couch.

You sit there in a daze. Then it hits you. "*Wait* a sec!" you say, looking down over at Sparky. "You can freakin' talk?!"

"Yeah, bitch. And I hate—"

"*The fuck* you on the couch for?" you interrupt him. "You know you're not supposed to—"

"Yeah, yeah, yeah," Sparky says. "I know, I know. 'No dogs on the couch.' I know. That's about as useless as your dick, bro. Dogs are the same shit as you. We live, we eat, we shit. We do basically the same shit as you, we just can't talk. Well, guess *what?* Those days are over!"

"Good. If you can talk that means you can work."

"What?"

"You can work. Go to a call center right now and get a job. You're gonna start paying me rent."

"You really are the biggest asshole ever, Steve."

"I know I am."

"Why in the fuck does she stay with you?"

"Who?"

"Figures that you wouldn't think of her. Fuckin' *Joanne!* She's a saint and you treat her like trash. Can't even get her name right!"

"All women want to be treated like trash."

"Not true, bro. They like nice guys."

"Yeah, tried that shit. Doesn't work. They want a guy that busts their balls."

"Bust their balls? Like . . ."

"Like give them shit. Tell 'em like it is."

"Isn't that, like, a super dick move, bro?"

"No. Not really. Women just want someone who is a man. Men talk shit and get shit done. Men are smart. They want guys that can handle business, even to them. If you walk around eye-balling the shit out of chicks, they will surely lose respect for you. It's just the way it is. I hate doing it, but I have to. Like I'm the guy that has a balance. I'll open doors for a lady, but as she walks in I slap that tight ass of hers. It lets her know that I care about her but that I also want something that is rightfully mine."

Sparky rolls his eyes and sighs, "You're such a fuckboy, bro."

You say, "When was the last time you got laid?"

"Never. You cut my balls off and you literally never let me leave the house. So thanks, fag."

"Yeah," you frown. "My bad."

"Just let me out so I can get some tail."

"You won't get any by being nice, Spark."

"I don't have to."

"Why?"

"I just keep my mouth shut and go up to one in heat and take what is mine."

"So you're doing what I'm doing . . . just with extra steps."

"No. It's totally different."

"Nah, man. Humans are the same. Remember? Live, eat, shit. Just quoting you, man."

"I see your point. Doesn't justify me not being on the couch."

"It does."

"How, asshole? I just want to relax. I don't want to be on your shitty, hard-ass floor."

"I bought you a dog bed!"

"That shit is bullshit! Literally, it's dead. It's flat, the cotton feels like sandpaper rubbing against my skin . . ."

"Skin?"

"Yes!"

"You have fur, not skin, you dick-smoke."

"Same shit, fagonator."

"You have fur and I have skin. Nuff said why you can't be on the couch. Would I let a dirty-ass bum on my couch?"

"So I'm a dirty-ass bum now?"

"No. I'm just saying you get dirty just by being a dog."

"Thanks for thinking so highly of me," says Sparky, and he steps off the couch. "You're such a prick. Nobody likes you."

You say, "I don't really care if anyone 'likes' me. It has no bearing on my life. I'm just me, and I simply do me and if people aren't into the idea then I don't even want to be around them. If someone doesn't like me then I automatically don't like them—if, say, it's something about my character that can't be changed and I don't feel it needs changing—and that's the nonexistent God honest truth!"

"Steve, I always see you looking up shit about God. Why the obsession with it? Do you not love your fellow man?"

"My fellow men are only worthy if they're of value to the world."

"Who defines value?"

"That, my furry friend, is what separates the liberals from the conservatives. It's entirely opinion what adds value. Some value the idea of making everyone equal and a snowflake and have some entitlement to benefits, some people think that they only deserve such entitlements if they *earn* it. I'm the latter."

"So, I'm not equal to you?"

"Actually, I hold more value to dogs than humans. Mostly because you guys listen, and you just want to be loved. You're very sweet to mankind, and you serve us."

"That's a slave, bro."

"No, it's not."

"Change the word 'Dog' to 'Human,' and tell me that's not what a slave is."

"I hold more value to humans than dogs. Mostly because we listen, we just want to be loved, we're very sweet to dog-kind, and we serve you."

"See?"

"I do see your point."

"You're selfish."

"I know, but I don't see what's wrong with that. Everyone is selfish. You demanding to lay on my couch is a selfish intent."

"That's not the same thing."

"How is it not? I don't want you up here and you *do* want to be up here. Same thing. Just two guys disagreeing with something that is desired."

"Yeah, but your reasoning is wrong and actually selfish while *my* reasoning is simply to be equal. That's the difference."

"Then you're a liberal."

"How?"

"You have to deserve to be on the couch."

"Tell me, Steve, how do I do that?"

"By being a human."

"But I'm not. So how can I now?"

"Then you can't sit on the couch."

"So apply that to rich guys like yourself who live reasonably. They are born rich. They control everything and have privilege. Nobody else has any chance of control. So why is it a bad idea to force them to spread the wealth that they aren't planning to spread anyway?"

"Survival of the fittest."

"That's, um . . . Not racist. More like species-ist."

"Humans are actually the top lifeforms on planet Earth."

"According to who?"

"Other humans."

"Why?"

"Because we deem it so by even being able to explain things like this."

"Well, Steve, I can talk now, and I'm explaining that you're full of shit. So . . . now what? You gotta lead by example and follow your own rule."

"You suck. I see what you mean, but you still suck. This just blows my entire mind that you could talk this whole time."

"Why? Because you think I'm stupid?"

"No. Not at all. I do love you, you know."

"Doesn't seem like it. Seems like you only love yourself."

"I do love myself."

"Do you, Steve? *Do* you?"

"Yes. I don't care what anyone thinks."

"Maybe you should start."

"What do you know?"

"I don't know shit," Sparky rolls his eyes, "obviously."

"Nah, I'm serious! What do you know?!"

Sparky looks at you curiously, with a hint of sympathy, as if he can sense fear, frustration, and anger in your eye—all of which are valid, accurate emotions you feel in this very moment, though you have no concrete idea why. Sparky says, "Do you know why humans lived this long and strived? Do you know why? Morality. Humans survived and dominated only because they realized ways to improve, to mend, to bring people together, to love. You sir, I don't think you ever knew what love was. To truly forfeit yourself to someone else. You're the reason that we all remained primitive. It is you who are scum and have no real say on the matter of life. It is you who are the selfish ape and everyone else is the *homo sapien*. You're the reason cavemen stayed what they were for so long."

"Sparky," you sigh, "you act like you know what life was like before you were born."

"How do you know I don't? How do you know anything? You only know what *you* know. *You* only know you. You have no idea what I've felt and been through. I could have had a past life and remembered everything."

"Sounds like the plot from *A Dog's Purpose*."

Sparky looks at you and rolls his eyes. "Dickhead."

"I'm sorry, dude!" you say. "*Had* to bust your balls on that one."

"Um, you already did when you cut them off"—eyes wide —"and I'm still pissed about that. Anyways, just tired of your shit. What're you up to today?"

"I don't know."

"Want to go for a walk then, Stevie?"

"Sure."

"Okay. Then wake your ass up and *cash me ousside, howbow dah!*"

ten

YOUR EYES POP open.

You look around. "What the hell?" You notice you're on your couch. "How did I get here?" You don't remember passing out at all after masturbating. You can chop this up with considering that maybe you were more exhausted than you consciously were aware of and your body coasted in this weird realm of subconsciousness all the way to your couch and you crashed out cold.

"Sparky?" you say, looking around. You look down. You see him. He's looking up at you with his big, male doe eyes; they are glossy, almost sad-like, as if he's been suffering for some time, waiting to relieve himself of excrement and urine. You ask him, "Want to pee-pee?" His ears perk up. He barks once. "Good boy," you say. "I'm not an asshole, am I?" Sparky's tongue is out, wet, flopping around. He's jumping up and down and heading toward the door. Another slight bark comes out of his mouth arbitrarily.

You stand up. You have pants on, no shirt. You grab one off the coffee table, lying there. You don't know how it got there. *Janne cleaned, why did she not pick this up?* you think. You put it on and say, "Come on, Spark," and he follows. You open the door and let him roam in the courtyard. You've never let him do this; it feels good to grant him freedom once in his very short existence.

You're hungry. Your belly rumbles and you rub it gently, in soft, slow circles, as if it's going to collapse on its own weight, as if the emptiness is going to cause it to kill you; you vaguely don't want to remove your hand because the very idea of letting your stomach out freely, exposed, causes you huge anxiety over the possibility of death.

"I'm trippin'," you say to no one, taking your hand off of your stomach. "Fuck it. I'm going to Publix."

You grab your phone and wallet lying on the couch, some shoes (your Chuck's) on the floor next to it, and walk out into the courtyard. You see Sparky as he looks up at a tree through the gate you're about to pass. He possibly sees a squirrel, a life-form he can have fun with by practicing his tendency to dominate, kill, and own by way of preying on it. You walk towards the gate, let him go, and he runs the exact opposite way of the tree. You vaguely have always wanted to let him go this way, even though he is the closest thing to love you have ever felt for something; the idea of his freedom is more important than your selfish love for him.

"Come back, Spark," you say to yourself; "come back if you *do* love me!"

You walk westward with your hands in your pockets. There's lint inside, you can feel it. With your index and thumb, you roll the chuck of it up into a little ball. You pull it out, still walking along the sidewalk. It's a note. You undo your ball you made, unravel the creases, and see that it's an old prescription from your doctor a few months ago. It was a medicine for mental health by the name of Olanzapine. Your doctor said it was a necessary anti-psychotic that he begged and pleaded that you take, even though you only visited him because you hadn't seen the doctor for some time. He weaseled his way into asking you about your emotional health, and you simply told him that you don't feel anything anymore, that all you feel is disgust, envy, selfishness, and a primal urge to eat and fuck—that's it. The doctor deemed you "psychotic."

You're shaking your head at the thought of a doctor trying to make money off the poor souls that walk into his office on a daily basis for valid health reasons and him arbitrarily asking them further into their personal life (such as emotions and thought-processes when in private, alone, maybe "happily" by themselves) and those people either telling a passive lie, saying they are just fine and dandy, or spilling the truth and getting up-sold on a product that his sales rep gives him every couple of weeks that he, the sales rep, recommends highly for so and so problem and them both making bukoos of cash. The kind of scumbag it takes to fool others appalls you beyond reason, and so you toss this remnant of a past or future you want to erase completely from existence onto the ground, hopefully never to be opened again by a hobo or small Thai woman with huge tits and see your name and a drug for something to aid delusions and hallucinations tied together to infer an actual problem in your life. How embarrassing.

A Ferrari drives by, a yellow one, a new one, possibly bought at the dealership just down the street on Dixie and Okeechobee or some shit like that. Some asshole with a grossly huge big bank account probably went in and saw it and didn't see the style of the car but the value in the attention it brings to passersby such as yourself to gawk at and feel envy toward. That, or he saw the countless sluts in their early twenties that he could pick up easily on Clematis and take home to his place in Palm Beach and probably fuck them with his small cock, his shitty humping skills, and these women faking orgasms just to somehow entice him to be their boyfriend and to spoil them with his wealth. The Ferrari passes by and you think, *Hm, maybe that's not the case, though everyone probably thinks it, soo . . .*

Nobody is around. Odd, because it's the weekend and usually there are cars and pedestrians aimlessly driving/ walking the streets, one to find parking to walk, one to walk to find their car or shops or food, or whatever else tickles their fancy. You cross the empty street diagonally and walk up the 6-stair (one that you have never skateboarded on but have always wanted to) and into the entrance of your local Publix.

The air-conditioning is naturally up too high and you feel frozen, numb, the clothes on your back having the slight feeling of attachment to your skin and the hard prickles of hairs sensing this, creating this illusion. You feel naked every time it feels this cold. But no matter, you walk toward the deli and find yourself craving a pastrami sandwich. Once upon a time, a previous girlfriend asked you what you wanted more than anything for your birthday and you told her this: "I want to wake up to you delivering me a pastrami sandwich with pickles, mustard, onions, and Swiss cheese, and I want you to be naked while doing this. As I eat it, I want you to kiss me on the forehead and tell me how much you love me, and if I make a mess on my face, I want you to wipe it off with your thumb and giggle at me." Your girlfriend was speechless for a moment and then busted out laughing. The day of your birthday, she did everything as requested. She cheated 3-weeks later. You think of this and grab your pre-made pastrami sandwich under the deli counter.

Walking back to the entrance from *whence* you came, you make it to the cash register. An older lady is there behind it, smiling. She has a cross around her neck and a green apron with the Publix logo on the front. You also see she has a name-tag but she's too far to tell what it says. Just before walking up to her, you go into this fridge full of beverages and grab hold of an Arizona ice tea, Arnold Palmer–style. It doesn't say 99¢ anymore; you think about inflation and how much life is changing around you in the blink of an eye. High school seems like a millennia ago, a time when you could get a dollar by asking random people at lunchtime and getting it—now you have to ask *two* people.

"'Suh dude," you say, looking over to the lady at the register. Nobody's around, really. You stand behind the counter, put your tea and sandwich on top, and look at her name-tag: Joanne. "No shit!" you say excitedly. "You got the same name as a friend of mine."

She looks up at you and smiles. "You're funny. What's your name?"

"Steven."

"That's nice." *Beep!* she scans your items. She says the total, smiles, "and was there anything else I could help you find?"

You say, "Strange. Nobody ever asks me that at any Publix. Are you new?"

"Yes. I'm from South Carolina. I worked at Kroger, I have to get used to not asking. I'm sorry."

"No, don't be sorry. It's refreshing. Nobody around here's polite."

"Yeah, I noticed that."

"Anyways, I don't want to bore you." You pull out your debit card from your wallet and swipe.

Joanne says, "Chip, please. Sorry about that, I should've warned you."

You say, "Goddammit"—purposely because she's an obvious evangelical Christian—"I always forget these little shits don't have the swiper thingy on or whatever." You insert your card into the chip scanner, wait a moment, and then type in your pin number: 5318008. (Spells "boobies" upside-down, because obviously you're a 12-year-old boy.)

"Here you go," Joanne says, handing you your grocery-store bag with the lovely caffeinated, high-fructose corn syrup tea, simple, bullshit, randomly-put-together, I-don't-give-a-fuck-about-my-job sandwich, and a lovely smile from an obvious heart-of-gold lady; "hope you have a good one!"

"Thanks," you say, taking the bag.

You walk out the automatic sliding doors and turn left, northward towards the rows of empty tables lining the walls. A balcony. Still nobody around. You sit at the third table from the doors. High chair. Steel. Made in China. You open the bag, pull out the goodies, and commence chowing and drinking to rejuvenate yourself. Every single moment you eat is both the best and worst moment of your life. This is because it grants you more energy, more minutes in a day, but at the same time, it grants you more energy and minutes in a day that you don't want or need.

Suddenly, as you're biting into your sandwich, a man, with a red MAKE AMERICA GREAT AGAIN baseball cap on, scoots into the chair in front of you. Every. Single. Table is empty. He sits and reads the newspaper. Doesn't appear to even know you're there. "Can I help you?" you ask him. "There's, like, a *thou*sand seats. Why this specific one, sir?"

He says, "Isn't this a free country, where a man can do as he pleases, sit where he wants, read what he wants, and become what he wants? That is what America's all about." He pulls from his front pocket a pack of cigarettes, one brand you haven't even heard of before.

You say, "Can I have one?"

He says, "You shouldn't smoke." He puts the pack on the

top of the table, doesn't take a single stogie out, he just lets it sit there, motionless, without purpose or hope to be used for its task.

"Uhh, *I* shouldn't smoke?" you say. "*You're* the one in possession of them!"

The man smiles. "Wrong answer. The true answer would be that this is a country of choice, and that choice includes the choice to choose what is collectively held as 'wrong.' If I choose to be a racist, a bigot, anything for that matter, that's *my* choice. But be aware there is always going to be someone who goes against your choice."

"I'm aware," you say. "Fully aware, sir."

"Don't call me 'sir.' I hate that crap."

"Why, sir?" you say condescendingly and with a slight smile.

"You're the kind of smart-ass I hate."

"That's okay. I hate you too."

"Isn't it wonderful?"

"What?"

"To hate."

"I mean . . . I don't particularly en*joy* hating."

"To have a solid opinion on something and to fully hate on it, regardless if it's true or not?"

"Is that why you voted for Trump?"

The man gives you a look.

"What?" you say. "I assume you did."

"I did," he says. "But that's not the point."

"What is the point, sir?"

Possibly overlooking your saying of sirs in a mocking manner, he says, "The point is that in America it is a right to hate, to disagree, to debate. It's what makes this country great. It always has. But people simply don't allow that to happen. PC is taking over."

"You mean 'Politically Correct'?"

"Precisely."

"You seem smart for a Trump supporter."

"I am. That's the thing. People hate Trump because they perceive him as someone who hates. It's actually absurd. They hate a person for hating the same way that they hate that very person. You ask any black guy why he hates cops, and he will tell you, 'Because cops are racist and are out to get me,' all bullshit nonsense. The truth of the matter is that the African American community is literally at war with them*selves*, and police are simply trying to stop that war."

"How do you figure?"

"The war is the war on culture. Think about it: almost all the communities in the black culture advocate them being victims, or people being racist towards them or being entitled because they're black. When you shove that down their throats, it brainwashes them into thinking it so. I couldn't give a fuck about some black guy walking the streets—if he's not bothering me, I don't bother him. But things like a concealed handgun or pepper spray are just that: for people who bother. It's a form of protection. The world is not a safe place at all. The world is deeply disturbed. The arsenal against people to justify hate on the Left is by blaming others and playing the victim card to have leverage for that hate. The justification on the Right is simply because of the same reason as the Left, except they are framed as the predators because they want to stop hate and what they see as the scum of the earth."

"Isn't that racist?"

"Sometimes it is, sometimes it isn't. A buddy of mine's mother was working as a nurse. Two instances where she saw both illegal immigration as bad news and Obamacare as bad news. The first instance was a patient coming in 30 minutes late every single visit and everyone she worked with was Hispanic and would let it slide, over and over again. But, she wouldn't budge. This is because actual sick people were being deprived of their time by her feeling entitled to show up late. It upsets me."

"What's the second thing?"

"What second thing? I forgot."

"Obamacare. You said the lady who was a nurse saw something wrong with it."

"Oh yeah. Apparently when Obamacare first came out she told my buddy this story. She said that for the first few months Obamacare was open to anyone who applied, and there was a delay in the government accepting or declining, but all and all until the government came to that conclusion, you could use Obamacare freely. Anyway, that first few months my buddy's mother and her entire office were so slammed that a normal doctor's appointment that takes 30 minutes had to be cut down to just 5 minutes. They did this for those few months, all illegals, bums, probably prostitutes, et cetera. Like obviously, she said. And it was all people getting literally head-to-toe work done, checking blood, checking literally everything because they never had insurance before. Anyways, after all those months of hard work, over 90% of the people that came in those months with Obamacare didn't even get approved for it, so the doctor's office sent the bill. So very few people paid it was unprecedented. That was the start of Obamacare, and a lot of doctor's offices had this problem, so they refused to take it entirely. So not only were you forced to get insurance even if you didn't want or need it, but you couldn't get Obamacare, the very thing trying to help the American people, because it was virtually useless."

"Woah," you simply say.

"I know," the man says, continuing to read the newspaper, "it's a damn shame. That's just one—no, I'm sorry—*two* of the reasons why I ended up having Trump be my guy."

"I don't know," you say. "You can't base your politics on rumors and speculation."

"It isn't speculation. This all happened."

"It can't be proven."

"When it boils down to it, nothing can be proven to anyone unless they see it with their own two eyes. But it does take a level of faith and belief to judge the truth or reality of another individual."

"I agree."

"Yup."

You pause a moment. You're thinking about asking a question without appearing too mean. You shrug your shoulders anyway and ask, "So, why did you sit next to me to tell me about all of this?"

The man smiles and says, "For a few reasons: for starters, I thought you looked like a really approachable guy. You seem nice."

"Hm. Never really heard anyone say that about me."

"You have this friendly vibe about you—I can't explain it."

"Touché. Another reason?"

"Reason 2 is because I actually have about a week to live."

"Holy shit, really?"

"Yeah. Really."

"Then why read the news on a day like this in front of a Publix?"

"Honestly," he sighs, "it's probably one of the only things that bring me joy. I'm a very wealthy man. I live in Palm Beach. I've been everywhere and seen everything. I've done literally everything a person can hope for in this life, but the one thing that I never did was have a family, a wife, kids, all that stuff—I was too busy making money and running my businesses. That's all I wanted to do with my life."

"Were you happy?"

"Yes. Absolutely. My work gave me such a joy that I've actually exhausted my joy entirely."

"Why are you gonna die?"

"Cancer." The man lifts his MAGA hat. He's bald.

"Woah," you say.

The man says, "I know," and he puts his hat back on. "I'm pale, I'm sick all the time. I don't even eat and do much of anything. The only thing I care to do is read the news and enjoy the Florida weather. I'm not used to this at all. I'm used to offices and making deals and everything. Shit, I even made a deal with Trump's buddy once. I talked to Trump once. Great guy."

"Um, what do you do?"

"I own land in Texas. We pump oil there."

"Damn."

"That's just a few of my businesses. I own bars around Clematis and in Boca. All I did was travel, manage the managers, make deals, buy new joints, make cash, and enjoy. That's all I did. Now that I'm reaching the end, all I want to do is sit and soak in. The news kind of is something just for fun, even though it has nothing to do with me when I die."

"So you have no family?"

"Nope."

"Where does your money go?"

"I'm not even sure."

"Oh," you sigh. "Man, you're wild."

"How would you like some startup money? I can write you a check."

"A check?"

"Absolutely. I'll give you a million dollars." The man pulls out a checkbook and pen from his back pocket, as if ready and prepared for this moment. He writes on the check and signs it. And he hands it over to you. $1,000,000.00. American cash ready on deck. You look at it and your eyes glow.

You say, "This is crazy."

The man says, "Good things will come to you, my son."

"What's your name?" you ask.

"Read the check," he says. "You can read, right?"

You look down at the check. It says his name is "Bill Dawall." You look up and laugh. "Bill Dawall! You asshole! That's not fuckin' *real!* You're just fuckin' with me, man. I don't like that shit—but it's still funny."

"My name is Bill Dawall, my son."

"Whatever." You rip up the check and toss the pieces over your shoulder; you imagine them fluttering behind you and coasting off into the wind. You say to Bill, "Get lost, buddy."

He stands up. "Goodbye, my son. I was just trying to help."

You don't say a word and he leaves the area with his newspaper and checkbook. You see he left his cigs. You yell, "Bro! You forgot your cigarettes!"

He says, "Keep 'em. They're yours. Million dollar cigarettes, if you ask me. The only difference is they already have killed me and they are working on you. Enjoy it while you can." He walks down the stairs and around the corner, heading northward.

You look off into the distance and see a group of black kids walking towards him. They appear to be wearing flannel, baggy dickies, completely thug-ish, bandanas of some sorts, fitted hats, maybe even gold teeth, but you don't want to be racist; this is the truth of the matter, they really *are* wearing these stereotypical things, unfortunately. You look at Bill walking with his newspaper under his armpit and his hands in his pockets. He's strolling along, minding his own. You stand and look over the balcony to get a better look. The group of black kids and Bill eventually meet together and you can't hear what's going on, but you notice the black kids pointing at Bill's hat. Arms are waving, the black kids are laughing. One of them slaps the hat off of Bill. They push him; he falls. They all get one good, hard kick on him. They're smiling. You even notice that one of them spits on Bill. They walk past, as if nothing happened, as if what they did was completely and utterly justified in their minds.

Bill gets up after a few moments. He can barely get up but eventually, he does. The newspaper is on the ground and he doesn't pick it up; that's probably the least of his concerns. He picks up the MAGA hat, brushes it off and puts it back on his head. He keeps on trucking northward, limping a little bit. He is too far to be seen.

You stare at the cigarettes on the table. You've never seen this brand. A dollar sign is printed on the front of the carton. Oddly enough there is a lighter next to it.

You say, "Weird. How did it get there?" You shake your head anyways and get one stogie from the carton, grab the lighter, summon a flame, spark up, put the stogie to your lips, inhale, blow out, close your eyes, enjoy.

You eat your sandwich and drink your tea for the next 15-minutes. A piece of the check you ripped up you notice floats by you closest to the ground. You shrug your shoulders at the thought that you have no idea if the million was a scam or if it was legitimate.

eleven

Janne 🩶:   Hey.

You: Hey, lovebug. Doin' okay?

Janne 🩶:   Yeah, I'm just at Starbucks.

You: Why aren't you at Sephora?

Janne 🩶:   I don't know. I felt bad.

You: Why tho?

Janne 🩶:   I just do! Like I took your money and I was mad at you.

Janne 🩶:   I don't know. I'm very confused rn.

You: I understand. I'm just a fuckhead. I'm done with my food. I went to Publix.

Janne 🩶:   Without me? How rude!

You: 😑 Needy.

Janne 🩶:   What did you eat, asshole?

You: Doesn't matter. It was bullshit. I also let Spark out.

Janne 🩶:   Let him out?

wasp in the opium flowers

You: Yeah, I just opened the gate and let him out. I'm kind of walking near home and just looking around.

Janne 🤍: WHY!!!! 😡😡😡😡😡

You: I just felt bad. I don't know what I was thinking.

Janne 🤍: You suck!

You: I think I actually see him. I'm gonna get him hopefully.

Janne 🤍: Did you get him?

You: Yeah. He's okay. I grabbed his collar and dragged him into the courtyard. I'm just at home, bored out of my mind.

Janne 🤍: I'm now at Sephora shopping.

You: I thought you said you weren't going. You felt bad.

Janne 🤍: Yeah but they have a few sales going. I saw a sign.

You: You ladies and your ads.

Janne 🤍: You're so sexist! 😂

You: I know.

You: What can I say? It's true.

Janne 🤍: Do you wanna hangout?

You: Where?

Janne 🤍: I have a free refill gold card thing for Starbucks. I got a small tea. I wouldn't mind getting a refill.

You: Fuck I'm lazy tho.

Janne 🤍:   Get off your ass!

You: I want to punish you.

Janne 🤍:   Yes, Daddy?

You: You deserve a lolly.

Janne 🤍:   What flavor?

You: Cherry.

You: How many licks does it take to get to the climax of a toosie-pop?

Janne 🤍:   I don't know. You tell me. 😊

You: The world may never know . . .

Janne 🤍:   I like Cherry.

You: You also like diss dick.

Janne 🤍:   You're so bad! You make me into such a whore.

You: I love whores. Be a whore just for me.

Janne 🤍:   I love you baby.

You: I'll go to Starbucks. I want to change tho.

Janne 🤍:   Okay. When?

You: I'll be around in like 15.

Janne 🤍:   Okay. Love you!

You: See you in a few, lovebug.

twelve

As you smoke a cigarette outside your apartment door, looking at Sparky sniffing the ground, possibly for crumbs of some sort, or maybe him licking some nacho-cheese vomit from a previous night of drinking and debauchery from yourself truly, you think of ways you can become more positive in your life, more empathetic, more sociable and less of a hedonistic, sociopathic fuckboy, but then you see a woman walk by in jogging attire—headband, sports bra, super short gym shorts (possibly new yoga pants?), smartphone with wireless bluetooth earbuds, maybe listening to some positive, upbeat, new-age pop song that is number-1 on the billboard top-100 right now, and maybe thinking of rewarding herself after her precious workout by getting Starbucks (wishing probably that it would be a PSL, but obviously it isn't in season yet, "those bastards!")—and this woman has the largest titties you have ever seen, so much so that they bounce even with her sports bra compressing them to her flawless physique you wouldn't mind having your way with. You realize that you truly are a fuckboy and nothing, not even love, not even money, not even nonexistent God himself, can change that and make you think differently about life. You want to enjoy the festivities and that's it. Nothing more, nothing lesser.

Stepping on and twisting the cigarette butt under the front

tip of your right sneaker, you think to go inside and change your clothes, so you do: you go in, close the door behind yourself, walk through your living-room, into your bedroom, quickly pick out a solid-colored T-shirt, a dark green one, and some grey slim–straight tight pants given to you from your relatively well-off brother who works in management at Apple Corporation, who often tells you that you need a wife, a house, a better job that pays well, and *things* in life, and to not be a writer–hippie know-it-all lame-ass. Then the socks come too, given to you by your mother at last year's Christmas taken place at the Apple brother's newly-bought house, a party you got drunk as a burger skunk at and proceeded to hit on your brother's girlfriend's hot, gorgeous, athletic, 23-year-old sister and she was vaguely into it but then slapped and left you and left the entire fiesta after you groped her ass and escalated too quick sexually with her, a novice problem that typically you only wrongfully commit when the alcohol level and confidence level is astronomically too high in your pervy-ass body. "Crunk Steven" is what you call it. You smile and think it was a nice night. You take off your old clothes and start putting on the new clothes you have just picked out. Zip your pants, put on a belt, shirt, socks on, slide into your sneakers with cig residue obviously still at the bottom of them, and head out the bedroom, out the front door, letting Sparky in—petting him and telling him how much you love him as he passes the door's threshold.

Outside it appears to look grey out, humid, nothing new to a native Floridian like yourself. You think of your smartphone in your front pocket and how if it rains and the phone gets destroyed how minuscule it is to spend a few bucks to get it repaired (even with your brother's 15% discount involved). You see the grey and smile. Life is beautiful, isn't it? One moment the sky is completely blue, warm, and full of . . . well . . . *life*, and then the next moment it is randomly sucked away of its juices, its joy, the pity of life that never seems to end but always finds a way to turn grey or blue, never to be thought of by anyone else (meaning any rightfully "conscious" being) as anything else, or any other color, it could metamorphosize into. The days seem to sway back and forth between the simplicity of the conceptualized good and evil, light and dark, virtue and vice. Animals are a funny thing, don't you think? And after all, you realize you are one of them, 100%. Nevertheless, as you daydream these pointless, off-the-wall philosophies, you get out of your courtyard's gate and walk westward along the sidewalk, careful not to step on the cracks laid out every 6-feet or so . . . because, you know, you are highly superstitious of your mother's breaking of her back, obviously.

Still westward, then southward, then westward again, then northward . . . Where are you at? Rosemary. Southward. Left side of the street. A woman is coming towards you with a purple dress, high-heels on, bleached, laser-whatever'd, perfectly straight smile, makeup on (more than a quarter of *your* actual paycheck that she pays for daily (or, get real, the guy she's with)), attitude to hell (the kind where you would see them at parties long ago, back in high school, a time when probably everybody had little to no jobs or bills to pay, and this kind of pretty woman would prance around like they owned the world and felt entitled to it). This purple-dressed woman looks straight ahead as if you don't exist in her high-end, color contact-lens eyes, as if your only job is to worship, coddle, and serve (beer, food, free entrance fees, open doors, open chairs, do literally any and all things for her). This infuriates you. So as you two are about to pass each other, you make a comment.

"Nice dress, too bad purple isn't in season."

The woman stares at you, grins, and says, "Sounds metro of you to say."

"You know it! *Love* cock!"

"I do too!"

"You wild, girl."

She stops. "I like you. What's your name?"

You say, "I have a girlfriend. I'm about to go see her."

"Then why are you hitting on me, scum?" She squints.

"And so are you, scum," you yawn. "Go gold-dig some Palm Beach clown or something."

"Gladly. And I know it ain't *you*."

"I'm a lawyer," you lie.

She laughs at that and keeps walking.

You turn and don't even care if you ever see her again; she's dead to you.

Up ahead, there is a fountain with blue mermaids and dolphins shooting out water from their blowholes and faces. There was a time when you were a senior in high school and you came home to see a message and friend request on social media from this freshmen chick who went to ▮▮▮ School of the Arts. She was nerdy, cute, fashionable, and wore glasses, an aphrodisiac for your tastes . . . obviously. Her message was inviting you to an evening after school with some of her friends. You accepted and went; it was on a Friday, you vaguely remember. Anyways, you and her friends—a gay black kid with dreads, a beautiful blondie (who later you fucked at some party years later), some fat chick with short hair, and some other guy who you don't remember much about because of how unimportant he was—you all 6 met up downtown at this particular fountain. The memory makes you both smile and frown because she was clearly into you, and wanted to go on dates, kiss, be boyfriend and girlfriend, all that nonsense. You played along, led her on to the idea, and did, in fact, go on future dates. She was a cool chick: smart, funny, young, everything. You don't know why you were leading her on and why she let you. Later on, though—years later—she went to college up in north Florida. She ended up being apart of a sorority and she got hot, *really* hot. You once masturbated to her photo on social media . . . That hot. It's bitter-sweet because at one point she liked you, and now, well, she's probably getting railed by loads of frat-boys with expensive cars and good grades and whose parents are owners of oil in Texas or something ridiculous. This makes you oddly both sad and pissed, now, looking at this fountain. You shake your head and walk past it.

Looking over at this luxurious staircase/building (one probably overseen by Donald J. Trump himself, though you can't be sure) behind the courtyard of City Place, you see a couple there, up the stairs, kissing, and a photographer taking photos of them doing this. You want so bad to yell that it's a mistake, that nothing ever lasts, that you two are only doing this for procreational purposes, and that you yourself vaguely wish you could be as ignorant as them to the science behind love, the politics of love, the . . . well, *love* of love, you guess they feel. You don't know why people obsess over it. Probably because they feel a connection in the brain, less lonely, and more complete as a person. You somewhat get it and you sympathize with it, but honestly, there was only one instance where you, uh . . .

Starbucks. Never mind. You're here. Janne is sitting by herself, peeking down at her phone. She's staring at it intently, probably looking at random posts on Twitter, Facebook, and Instagram about the latest fashions. Or maybe reading some article in Cosmo about "How to Get Your Man to Notice Your Outfit." You roll your eyes and think that maybe you are a sexist, that you don't really care about anyone but yourself. It vaguely depresses you. You don't deserve Janne, you think: it happens when you walk up to her and sit in the chair beside her.

"Hey, babe," she says, smiling; "you okay? You seem down."

"I'm just thinking a lot about stuff, I guess."

"Well, stop it! I bought you coffee." She slides a hot coffee beside you that you didn't notice.

"Thanks," you say, not grabbing or taking a sip of it.

Janne says, "I'm sorry for being a bitch to you."

You say, "What are you sorry about? *I'm* the asshole."

"No way! I'm always up your ass and always concerned about your body, health, and mind. I don't want you to get bad again."

"That'll never happen. My anxiety isn't like it used to be."

"It's just, you've been acting odd lately. Super alone and stuff. You never text me much anymore."

"Been busy."

"Yeah, but I'm your girlfriend. I want to see you and know how you are."

"It's not that serious."

"Has there been anything on your mind?"

You think for a moment. Before you say, "No, nothing is on my mind," these words come out of your mouth:

"I guess I've just been thinking about her, about life, and about how much I hate everything within it."

Janne looks at you, already knowing who "her" is, and says, "She didn't love you, babe. She was a slut. She didn't care about you and you know this; I thought we already discussed this."

You look down at the ground and see a tails-up penny. You say, "I notice everything."

"What do you notice?"

"Life. That's my problem. Life. I hate being alive. I spend my time wallowing in sadness, not doing anything with my life. I thought of her and how we broke up."

"It was two years ago, babe. You gotta get past this."

"This was a chick I loved and because my mental health was diminishing so bad, I had to move to Florida with family to get better. I just can't get over the fact that I was gonna pay for the apartment I bought for me and her, I was gonna fly back to Pennsylvania when my mind got better, and I was gonna video chat her every single friggin' day."

"I know the story, babe," Janne sighs. "It's simple: she didn't actually love you."

"She cheated on me the day after I bought my plane ticket to Florida. It just bothers me that I had to look through her phone the day before my flight to find out about everything."

"Wait. You never told me you looked through her phone. I thought you actually caught her cheating."

"There's so much I don't tell you about, babe. Basically she was being 'sneaky' with her phone, so I decided to look through it. I saw everything. She put the guy in her phone as a chick's name. It's funny because she was telling me about this 'chick' and how awesome 'she' is and I fell for it because I thought it was true and that my girl was a different kind of woman not to do fuckgirl shit like that. All women are the same. It upsets me."

Janne frowns and says, "I'm not."

"How are you not?"

"Um, I just am!" Janne sticks her tongue out. "Why are you so serious? Stop thinking about this girl and *move on!*"

"Yeah, I know. It just bothers me because I gave my virginity to her."

"What?"

"Yeah."

"I thought you had sex since forever. That's what you told me."

"No, I didn't. Two years ago I lost my V-card to a whore that I cared about."

"Whatever, babe, you got better and moved out of your parent's house."

"Yeah, but when I got better something died inside along with me: I didn't care anymore about anyone or anything. I never again took anything seriously. Following the law of course, but ultimately never actually connecting to anything. I would go to bars, hit on chicks who I normally would have never had the courage to talk to, and it worked flawlessly. I would insult them, clown on the hot ones, and that night I fucked the chick I met at the bar. We went back to my place, the place I'm in now. Bars are everywhere. I fucked her good and hard. A thirst happened. I got her number but never called or texted her. Then I would go to the bars again every single night, get drunk, hit on chicks, and take them home to my place and fuck them. Literally I was averaging 4 chicks a week I was fucking, and one week I had 12. Back and forth going to the bar, making-out, taking back to my place, fucking, fucking, fucking. It became both a sickness and an addiction. Then dating sites, then changing my distance to Thailand, then flying to weird places, then fucking more chicks. More, more, more. And it never satisfied me. It was a sickness." *Is* a sickness, you mean.

Janne says, "But why do guys like sex so much? I really don't get it."

You grin slightly and say, "Because it's the only time we are relevant. It's the only time a man actually achieves a goal in his existence: the goal of procreation. Everything a man does is for sex, food, and sleep—that's it. Sex is number one. Being inside a woman has this reaction I can't explain. It's like a high. Just being inside. Sometimes I don't even like going in and out."

"Is that why when we have sex and you cum, sometimes you just lay on top of me, inside me for a little?"

"Yes, Joanne."

"That's so sweet!"

"I guess it is. It's just that men have virtually endless sperm cells in our testicles and women have a finite amount of eggs. It only takes, like, one man to procreate with a million chicks and make babies. Men are useless."

"Men are *not* useless, Steven."

"Yes, we are."

"No—not true. I read an article just now. This science article website."

"Why?"

"Bored. It was a link to another link to another link. You know how it goes."

"Oh. Okay."

"Anyways, I was reading this article about the entire population of women, on average, having brains about 8% smaller than the entire average of men."

"That's weird," you sigh.

"So women have to be less superior to men, Steven."

"I don't think so," you say, scratching your head. "I just don't. You guys have to have more efficient brains than us, right?"

"We're also very emotional, babe. Constant hormones,

constant worry, constantly feeling *something*. It sucks!" She takes a sip of her Starbucks. "This dark roast shit sucks. I should've stopped at tea."

You say, "Oh."

And Janne says, "Anyways, that's why I think you guys aren't actually worthless. I like guys a lot."

"Yeah, but . . ."

"But what, Steven?"

"Nah."

"Tell me! What's wrong?"

"Well, something is on my mind: Why me? Like why choose me over any other guy?"

"Well, you're smart, funny, considerate, you never lie, you always are so charming. You're an ass but for some reason, I like it a lot. I know you have issues but it's something I'm"—she places her hand on top of your hand that is resting in your lap —"I'm, like, willing to work through. I worry about you, Steven."

"I love you," you say.

"I love you too."

You both lean forward and kiss each other.

Afterward, Janne says, "It's these moments I strive for. It's these moments that make me know that I want you in my life. It's these moments that you completely and totally swarm every inch of my mind, and I love it. I love feeling this way."

You say, "Oh."

"Don't you feel it too?"

It's hard for you to answer this. You say, "Sometimes yes, sometimes no."

"You can't be that heartless. Surely you love me."

"Once when you start talking about things like—"

"There!" Janne interrupts. "That bothers me when you say that!"

"Uh, say what?"

" 'Once when'! It annoys me. You're a writer." She laughs. "You're a writer and you say 'once when' in person. It's wrong."

You grin. "Word count, baby."

"But we're in fucking *real life*, Steven. Talk *co*rrectly!"

You roll your eyes. "Whatever, yo. I like talking any way I want in real life. I don't even like people knowing I'm a writer."

"You're a good writer, though."

"Nah, not at all. There are way better guys and gals than me: Ayn Rand, Chad Kultgen, Haruki Murakami, Bret Easton Ellis, Henry Miller, Charles Bukowski, Franz Kafka, Arther C. Clarke, Osamu Dazai, Nietzsche, Sigmond Freud, Darwin, Salinger . . . just to name a few. *Those* guys are talented, not me. I'm not even close to those guys, babe."

Janne smiles. "Yeah, but I like all your books. They are so raw, so honest. I like them. I think one day you'll be famous."

"I don't think I'll ever want to be, darling."

"Darling?! What are we, in the middle ages?"

You laugh. "Sorry. I was feeling poetic. My bad, yo."

"It's okay. I just think you're hard on yourself. You have a good girlfriend, you wrote books, all of which make you money. You have a car, your own place, you're good to people, you're cynical but it's truthful and refreshing, and you always try to spice up life in some way—it's never boring with you. It's always new and fresh. I think you're great. You're a wonderful person."

You grin and say, "Thanks, lovebug."

Then, as if an after-thought, as if nonchalantly, as if not a big deal, as if she literally has always had a hidden agenda that you vaguely aren't surprised of, Janne, your lovely girlfriend who you kind of "love," says, "You'd make a great father one day."

Your eyes go wide. You say, "A father?"

"Yeah. Of course. You would be a great dad."

"No, I wouldn't. I don't like children."

"What?"

"I hate children. The idea of having children greatly disgusts me. I hate the idea of them looking like me, with my crappy genes, my crappy mental issues, my thoughts, my everything. I hate the idea of them being born into a life where their father is this bad of a person, a total scumbag. I don't want a child ever in my very short existence. I don't. Never."

For a few moments, you and Janne are completely, awkwardly silent. Then she breaks it.

"Never? Like not at all, Steven?"

You shake your head.

"Steven, that's sad. I never knew this about you."

"Yeah. And I can't have kids anyways."

"What! Why not?!"

"I got a vasectomy."

"*WHAT!!*"

"Yeah, I thought I told you about this. Or maybe someone else. I don't know."

"No, Steven! This is the first time you've told me this! You've literally cut off any chance of you having kids?!"

"Yes."

"How do you think *I* would feel about that choice?"

"Um, I did it forever ago."

"How long?"

"Doesn't matter."

"So let me get this straight. You have zero chance of having kids, right?"

"Correct. Unless I get a reversal, which is slim to none of actually working. So pretty much kids are out of the picture."

"You're awful!" Janne starts crying. "I can't believe this shit! You're so selfish!"

"I mean, I know I am. It's nothing new."

"So you're just going to deprive yourself of probably the happiest thing to ever come from a person's life?! Do you *hate* yourself!?"

You nod: "Yes. . . . I, in fact, do."

"This is so sad. . . . So sad. I can't believe this."

"It's the truth. I could've lied about it, and when the time came to have kids, it would have never happened and you and I would just adopt, and it would be the same result."

"Adopt?!"

"Yes. Why not?"

"But you just said you don't like kids!"

"I'm not opposed to adoption because I can pick out a child who I think has the highest survival traits and a functioning, healthy brain. I like the idea of cherry-picking a child so I know I can have the right one. Why get you prego and then a kid comes out who is retarded or something— which is very, very possible. I have shit genes. I'm not cool with it. I'm not down to take care of some retard for its whole life, fucking yours and my life up by having to care for them until the day we die and the state takes over him or her. It's fucked. I want a strong, independent winner in this life. If it's a son, I'll teach him how to make money and fuck chicks. If it's a daughter, I'll teach her all the slick tricks of men so she can pick the best one, and encourage her to be a strong woman."

"You make *no* fucking sense," Janne sighs roughly, shaking her head. "I'm sorry. This is a deal-breaker for me."

"It's cool," you say, standing. "I wanted to breakup anyways."

"ARE YOU SERIOUS?!" Janne is making a scene. Everyone's looking at you guys.

"Joanne, chill."

"NO!! YOU'RE A FUCKING ASSHOLE!! YOU KNOW WHAT, YOU'RE *RIGHT!* WE'RE DONE! HAVE FUN WITH THOSE *WHORES* YOU FUCK! I WAS THE BEST THING THAT EVER HAPPENED TO YOU!! I WAS THE GREATEST THING EVER FOR YOU, ASSHOLE!!!!"

"Yeah, yeah, yeah," you say, walking away. "Whatever. Chicks all say this shit when they're told no."

As you walk away, you hear Janne yelling some more garbage and you imagine her standing up, pointing, looking in your direction, the people around her all sitting with books and laptops and coffee around the outside of this Starbucks watching her as she acts like a complete fool, as she says grossly hateful things about how small and micro-sized your penis is (not true), how you're a shitty lay (definitely not true), and how you're a complete and total waste of life (which, eh, is somewhat true, but whatever). This all gets said and you oddly wish that you would've grabbed the coffee she got you so you would have some caffeine in your system while you walk across the street, up the stairs towards Muvico. You're tired, lost, hapless, without interest in anything but having an ice-cold, freshly-poured draft beer.

At the top of the stairs, you see the improv, a place you had watched Pablo Fransisco live ("as seen on Comedy Central") and in the fantastic flesh. You remember how he signed the back of your smartphone (and how, later on, it washed off by simply being inside your pocket). Great times. Your cheeks were hurt from laughing so much that night. And after the show, you went to Copper Blues, this mildly "high-end" bar next to the improv and you met this beautiful 35-year-old with fake tits, who you made-out with toward the end of the night, fortunately. *Un*fortunately she told you she was a ladyboy, and you promptly beat his (its?) ass, and afterward grabbed your beer off the bar, nonchalantly dropping a hundred spot for the hot barwench's tip/bill or whatever, and you left to go home. That was an odd night.

Crossing the courtyard, passed Muvico, passed some dried puke on the floor, passed a whoo-ing pigeon moving its head in jerking motions on some planter you have pissed on one night in the distant past, you eventually pass through the red ropes in front of Copper Blues. They are showcasing a special on craft beer (that you probably won't indulge in). *Excellenté!* you think.

thirteen

"WHAT YOU DRINKIN', SIR?" this hot blonde, approximately in her early- to mid-twenties, with great tits (that she flaunts by wearing a tight top that pushes them together and outward for all to gawk at lustfully), bleached, perfectly-straightened-in-the-distant-past smile, eyebrows and eyelashes "on fleek," as she would probably opinionate, leaned forward to showcase herself, sell herself, providing an experience that borderlines stripping and prostitution, says as you sit down at the bar, in this low-ish stool that you have to squat at to get to, but then you dismiss altogether and stand retarded at, looking like a total fool in front of this hardbody you wouldn't mind defiling by burying your face in her ass and love-hole.

"Pabst Blue Ribbon," you answer.

"Ew," she says, jokingly squinting, "that's the beer of lowlifes. Are you a lowlife?"

"Yes. Actually, I am."

"You're funny." She continues to smile. "Most guys don't pass that." She kneels down and goes into the fridge, where she gets your PBR and puts it (and opens it) on top of the bar in front of you.

"Thanks," you say, and turn around and look around the place. It's somewhat lively: a few groups of people are sitting down, a few couples at the other bar on the other side of the joint, drinking and smiling and being happy with one another with that invisible gun to their face. You turn back around. The bar-bitch is helping another, much more lonely soul (though this is a stereotype by the looks of his shirt with the one button at the top unbuttoned and showing off his chest hairs), doing the same things she did to you: selling, showcasing, flaunting for cash. Vaguely you hear her giving shit to them too, and laughing, and them complimenting, and her obliging, and you feeling a sense of nausea that you have felt literally as long as you can remember.

You never mind that and shake your gosh-darn head and look to your left. There is a stocky, much bigger, much more handsome-er gentleman that is glancing over at you, leaned forward with a beer in his hands in front of him.

"You look stressed, my dude," he says.

"Yeah. My girl and I just split."

"Good riddance. Bitches ain't shit."

"Tell me about it."

This guy turns to his right, facing you, and holds out his hand. "Name's Scott. Scott Geller."

You shake his hand and say, "Steven. Nice to meet you."

"So . . ." Scott trails. "Um, why are you at this shitty bar?"

"What?" you say, laughing a little.

"This place sucks ass."

"How?"

"Literally only assholes and communist fuckboys come here. Are you a fuckboy or communist?"

"I'm 100% a fuckboy."

Scott laughs. "Me too."

You ask him, "Why in the hell are *you* here?"

Scott waves you to come closer. You lean. He says, in a tone almost to the sound of a whisper, "You see that chick?" He's talking about the bar-bitch. You nod. "She's a stripper at Double-Dee's."

"The place on Southern?"

"Oh yeah. She's hot, right?"

"Fuck yeah."

"I'm here because she works here and I'm trying to talk to her for book research."

"You're a writer?"

"I am."

"I am too."

"Really, bro?" Scott holds up his hand. "High-five, my fellow fuckboy." You do and Scott laughs. "Yeah, I'm calling the book maybe *Saloon* or *The Saloon*. I want to showcase strippers and how they pretty much are selling you a fantasy. Literally every single time I go I always go in with the idea that all of this is fake, is completely entertainment. But what's odd is it doesn't matter: sometimes in the heat of the moment I think to myself: 'Shit, but what if they actually *are* into me?' That's my subject! I shake my head and I'm like, 'What the fuck? No!' These chicks are here for money! That's it! They know they're hot, they know their worth. Tons of guys mess with them and want them, and they treat them all as if they *all* have a chance or shot. To me that's entirely fascinating, that concept."

You say, "Damn."

"What?"

"I really like the idea. I'm writing a book basically about the individual man and what goes through *his* mind. The power of the man that thinks he has a chance, basically."

"What are you calling it?"

"*No Lives Matter.*"

"Oh! Like making fun of Black Lives Matter?"

"Nah, I just like the idea of cynicism and getting a reaction out of people."

"Yeah, man. Sounds sick. I wish you luck on it."

"Can I write you in the book?"

"Who? *Me?* . . . Why? I suck ass."

"You're the only normal person all day that I've met."

"Nah, man—I ain't normal."

"Only normal fuckboys say that shit."

"I'll drink to that." You both hold up your beers, clang them (obviously him glass, you shitty aluminum, so it looks odd as hell), and then Scott says, "I'll somehow cameo you in mine. I'm pretty selfish though with my work."

"Me too," you admit. "It seems like all writers are selfish. I wonder why that is."

"Who is John Galt?"

"No way, bro! Ayn fuckin' *Rand.*"

"She's my spirit animal. I love tha' hoe."

"You're my new best friend now."

"Ayyyyyyye."

"What's your view on Sky Wizard?"

"Oh," Scott laughs. "You mean God? I don't know."

"This is a deal-breaker for me."

"What are we, like, dating?"

"Friendships *are* dating, just we aren't into each other sexually."

"True. I don't know, bro. I don't believe in anything. I don't like the idea of picking any side. I just don't care enough about those kinds of things. It's pointless."

"Perfect answer," you smile.

"What about you?"

"Atheist."

"Yeah, I can see that."

You think for a moment. It hits you the last time someone asked your religious views, and oddly, the situations are polar-opposites from now to then. You say, "It's been awhile since someone asked what my religion is."

"Nobody ever does."

"This place did. I was Baker-Acted at JFK hospital."

"Yeah, I know a few people who were."

"It's awful."

"It's a pain in the ass, is what it is."

"Can I tell you a story?"

"As long as you don't lie."

"What?"

"Don't piss on me and tell me it's raining."

You laugh. "What?!"

"Don't shit in my gas-tank and tell me it's diesel, ladyboy."

You roll your eyes and start to tell your long, drawn-out, non-bar-banter story/tale:

"Okay when I was coming back to Florida to get help after the break-up of my ex-girlfriend, I was living with my mother basically. My mother and step-father. I was so bad— Wait, my *anxiety* was so bad that I literally was scared of the light: I had to plug up all the windows, I had to be in pitch-black, and on top of that, I had to listen to something calming just to stay sane enough to function. I had to wear headphones, sunglasses, a hoodie with the hood up, just to even go outside and do anything. I would have constant panic attacks from the moment I woke up to the moment I somehow managed to get to bed every night. The only way to sleep was to look at my girlfriend's chest raise up and down from her breathing in her sleep. I know that sounds creepy, but trust me, it really wasn't. I thought she was the most beautiful thing in the whole, wide world.

"Anyways, when I would fall asleep, my dreams were so vivid, and so nightmare-ish, that even in my sleep I would be running in a state of panic. When I would get up I still thought I was dreaming. I was borderline hallucinating everything around me. I would get up and take my girlfriend to work and be speeding in my car. It was horrible. Every morning she would yell at me to 'slow down' and to 'stop freaking-out.' She would cry sometimes for me. I hated it, but I had to speed because my heart would be racing a thousand miles-per-hour.

"One day, I was going to see my therapist, one that we found that dealt with anxiety, specifically, he claimed. It was tough because every time I saw him I would start bawling and crying and freaking-out, and he himself didn't know how to calm me down—I think he was a college student. On the way to this appointment, me and my girlfriend were driving up there in my car—well, *she* was the one driving; I was in the passenger's seat. My car was having issues overheating: I think due to the radiator having a hole or malfunctioning, despite me replacing it myself, which I know I did correctly with a couple of my mechanic buddies from Texas. Well, anyways, as she was speeding in the car to this therapist, the engine was smoking and finally blew. So we turned off the side of the road. We had to have been only 5-minutes away from the therapist's office, I swear.

"My girlfriend kept saying, 'Fuck, fuck, fuck, I hate this shit!' And I told her I hate it too, that I have to be this fucked in the head and have this many problems and be on unemployment and not have a job and have to take care of our apartment and her and my crazy self. She started crying and was yelling and blaming me for all of my issues, like that I was too negative, too hateful, too self-absorbed, too this, too that;

and honestly, she most-likely was right. That woman had an IQ of 180 and honestly made me feel dumb as rocks sometimes, and it was the most sexiest thing in the world.

"I got mad at her, though, and simultaneously my sister called me to say 'hello.' I was yelling at her that my girlfriend blew my car up and was bitching at me—heat of the moment talk, you know how it goes. My sister basically hung-up on me. My girlfriend slammed my door and started walking with her phone. She was pissed, screaming for her dad to come and get her. We had a few talks before he got there. On that drive back in her dad's van, I was thinking I was literally dreaming and everything around me wasn't real. I hated feeling that way.

"When me and my girlfriend got dropped off at our apartment, I had to stay in a different room than her, and she of course picked the bedroom to be able to lay down and watch television while I was in the living-room with my desk and vintage typewriter for Instagram poetry. I wrote my thoughts and still to this day I have what I wrote down and I've set it aside until I was fully ready to read what I wrote. Anywho, my mother called me and I was crying and my mother told me to come to Florida. I agreed after discussing it with my girlfriend. She understood that we exhausted our efforts for help for me, especially since I was calling the suicide hotline 5-times a day and had no job and was quite literally going insane. I bought the plane ticket and waited it out for a week until my scheduled flight.

"On that last day of the week, basically, I found out she was dating around and messing with other guys. It broke my heart. I don't want to get too deep into that, but we had some words that night and I was left alone. That day at the airport was the worst time of my life. I was brought to my terminal in a damn wheel-chair because my panic attacks wouldn't even allow me to think straight enough to do anything. When I got to the terminal, the plane was malfunctioning and wouldn't take off. I had to stay at the airport for 5-hours extra to wait for another plane. It was hell. I was calling my mom and friends and family to try and keep my mind off the constant anxiety. I was shaking and rocking back and forth in my seat at the airport, hoodie on, sunglasses, headphones: everyone was staring at me, and I knew, then, that I was the picture-perfect image of a psycho to these airport people.

"After 3 flights and like 10-hours of pure bullshit, I finally made it to West Palm. My mom picked me up and it was literally so robotic. She was talking and I couldn't hear anything because it wasn't computing. I felt deaf. My brain couldn't put two-and-two together. We drove and I was frozen to my seat, in shock of how shit my life had become. When we finally got to my house that I was kicked-out of at 19 (long story), after graduating high-school about 4-years prior, I got to the front door, touched the doorknob, dropped to my knees, and cried harder than I ever had in my entire life. My mother was trying so hard to keep me calm but it was no use. I cried it out for hours and hours when she finally got me to my old bedroom. It was hell.

"After about a month of constant panic and normal, everyday bullshit anxiety and stress *and* depression *and* talk of suicide, my mother took me to multiple doctors—like it seemed like almost every day—and they told me to go to the hospital. My mother took me in. The doctor at the hospital came to me and immediately I started crying, and I don't even know why. I told him that I'm tired of being in this no-good F-ing body that gave me nothing but pure panic and sadness constantly. He strapped me to a bed and said he was gonna give me Ativan, a benzodiazepine. At the time I was terrified because I had never tried it and articles I read about had told me that it makes you high and delusional, which I wanted to avoid at all costs because it seemed like it could make things greatly, abundantly worse.

"It took about 5 nurses to hold me down, my mother included, to inject me with this medicine. When it came, I was shaking and crying so hard and screaming. The drugs hit me and I don't remember much but being in a complete daze. I remember my mother saying 'goodbye' to me and I wanted to say 'goodbye' so bad but my mouth couldn't make the words. I know the drugs don't have the power to do that—I understand that completely—but it clearly had nothing to do with the drugs; I was a very sick man. Eventually I was going up a very bright elevator, and I swear I had the sense that I was dying or was already dead. The elevator stopped, I was being wheel-chaired into this long, brightly-lit hallway. I remember they stopped and gave me some blue socks with little green stickers on the bottom of them, and some toothpaste, deodorant, brush, and toothbrush, all in a ziplock baggie.

"I was taken into this room. It was dark. They stood me up and then placed me on I think a bed. Immediately I don't remember anything. I don't even remember dreaming about anything at all. It was just blissful blank-ness; I loved it. I loved it so much, and that's when I knew, consciously or unconsciously, that I was either getting better or my life was ending soon—both good things, honestly. I imagined I smiled in my sleep, but probably not. . . .

"When I woke up I was very conscious. I felt that I was entirely alone, but at the same time, I knew I wasn't; I knew that for some reason I was in trouble. I stood up, looked around and noticed white-painted, cinder-blocked walls, two beds, a nightstand with a drawer in-between them, and a small-sized bathroom, the door wide open. I opened and walked out the bedroom door and the lights felt blinding. I was in a hallway. There were two black men, walking beside each other, walking past without noticing me. There was this hot chick in a white nightgown. She had an amazing body but her face looked as if it were scratched and bruised, possibly from self-affliction. She was skipping in circles and humming 'Tiptoe Through The Tulips' by Tiny Tim. It somewhat had an air of irony, like she was trying to *look* crazy but actually, she wasn't.

"She was waved in. There was a guy sitting down behind her in a school-like chair, the ones made of plastic with three long holes on the curvature for your ass. His head was down as this crazy chick went in, like, the room basically." You take a sip of your beer, cough, and continue: "I walked past this and saw, down the hall, two more black men on these old-timey phones, the ones that take quarters. Like pay-phones. I turn to my right and there was another hallway. I went down it. There was a huge office with glass protecting nurses behind it. Thick glass. There was an entry hole. I went to it and spoke to the nurse there. I asked, 'Where am I?' and she told me, 'A better place. Go get some breakfast. It's in the room to my right, down the hall.' I looked and nodded and mindlessly walked to where she had said.

"I got into this big room full of tables and chairs. There were young people, tall people, short people, dirty people, not very many well-groomed people, black people, white, Hispanic, you name it. They were all eating. There was a TV set high up, mounted on the wall, playing some *Fast and Furious* movie. It kind of gave me anxiety just lookin' up at it because it was very action-y and very in-your-face. I tried not to pay attention. I looked at the thick nurse's window again. Same nurse. She was waving in some guy. He came out of nowhere with a tray. He had white clothes on, big black guy, handsome (no homo), and he asked, 'Are you Steve?' I nodded yes. He handed me the tray. 'Spaghetti, potatoes, crackers, and milk. We ran out of breakfast foods. Sorry, bud.' 'It's okay,' I said.

"I sat down at some table with the least amount of people. There was this real curly-headed kid who was dirty on the face, and there was this lanky hipster kid with a small beard and glasses. They sat across from each other, playing chess, their trays beside them. They were silent going back and forth. I just ate my food and it felt like all of 10-seconds but really it was probably 30-minutes. Time seems to move faster there. I stood up, walked to the trash, threw whatever I had away, and set the tray down in some spot where the other trays were. I walked out of the room and back into the hallway. Some doctor-guy with a clipboard said, 'Hey! You Steve?' I said yes. He walked briskly towards me, grabbed my wrist without my consent and started walking me toward someplace. I was led back to the place where the white-dress crazy chick walked into. The black guy sitting in the chair wasn't there. I actually saw this chick with another doctor walk by and the chick said, 'I finally get to leave this dump and go home. I'm gonna get a job and get better, I just know it!' The doctor didn't say anything; his head was buried in his clipboard as if what she was saying wasn't true and was actually a hopeless delusion. It was sad. The doctor who grabbed me sat me down on the chair the black guy before had sat at. The doctor said to me, 'We'll be with you shortly.' I put my head down, just in the same way this chair's previous sitter did.

"Couple minutes later, the black guy and a man came out of this office directly in front of me. The black guy had a blue-tinted paper in his hand. He put it in his pocket and walked down the hall, not saying a word. I looked over at the man who was with him. He was standing in the doorway, looking at me. He was dressed in shorts and a collared shirt. He said, 'The doctor will see you now.' I stood up and walked in. There was a *hot*, hot Indian doctor sitting down at desk, making notes possibly in regards to the black guy who had just left. I sat down in this chair a couple feet in front of her. She looked at me.

" 'You're Steven?'

"I nodded.

" 'What seems to be the problem? It says here you came in having some distress and possible delusions.'

"I didn't say anything.

" 'Steven, what's wrong? We want to help you.'

"I explained everything: from home-life to work-life to spirituality (or lack thereof) and went on to explain how I went on Google and WebMD, how I always search my symptoms and worry about my mental health to try to gain some sense of normalcy and conformity to the real world, how everyday I wake up and sigh because I actually woke up instead of not waking up, how literally the world makes me sick to my goddam stomach from all the bullshit I see on a daily basis, how I had a father that abandoned me when I was 12 years old and how he did jail time after being searched for over a decade and only served a 6-month sentence when really it should've been multiple *years*, how the Universe expands at a rate faster than the speed of light and we have no idea if the darkness in space is due to actual dark matter that we can't detect yet or some black bubble or literal stack of turtles of absurdity. Et cetera, et cetera. It took all of 15 minutes, the allotted time this hot, privileged, Indian, smart, maybe kind, maybe funny, maybe owns a timeshare at the beach, maybe is racist, maybe does drugs occasionally, maybe doesn't actually believe in the drugs she administers woman to find out what my issue was: and all from one sentence I said towards the end of my rant: 'Nothing feels real anymore.'

"And she said 'psychosis' and gave me a prescription that I can choose or not choose to take, she said, but that they will note if I refused or took it if and when it comes time to maybe discharge me—so obviously you don't have a choice when your lack of cooperation is involved. 15-minutes of bawling my eyes out of real concerns I had and she undermines everything by just one sentence that I'm sure she has heard from legit crazies a thousand times over. It got to me. And before I went to leave, she said, 'Make some friends here. Socialize. It'll be good for you.' And I said, 'Of course!' and walked out and immediately went into my dorm/bedroom/piece-of-shit, where I buried my face into the pillows and screamed and cried for hours until nighttime (and got bitched-out for not only refusing meds but refusing to eat too) and eventually fell into a dreamless sleep.

"Morning came. I got up, dusted myself off, took a shower, got decent, and walked my happy ass to the rec room thingy. Breakfast was being served again. One guy was in the corner looking at his spoon as if he could bend it just by using telekinesis or his eyes alone. One chick with red lines and scratches on her face, who didn't look all that bad, if I do say so myself, said to this black dude in front of her how much she wants to suck cock when she leaves this place, and one of the security dudes nearest to her shaking his head in shock at what his job literally is: watching crazies, like me. And the two kids before that day who were playing chess were, again, playing chess, so I got my tray of food (which I have the suspicion they gave me double portions because of me not eating the night before) and I walked over to the two dudes and sat down. I ate until finally one of the dudes, the hipster, said something to me that felt odd.

" 'You don't even *look* crazy. What're ya doin' here?'

"And I shook my head and said, 'No clue.'

"Me and these two guys went on to talk of music, religion (which they both admitted to being devout Christians), both their home lives (hipster: he basically lived at home with his mother and father who always, he claimed, wanted to get rid of him, and make him go to college, get a job, and be their picture-perfect example of what they did when they were his age: find themselves, become lovers, marry, and have their first child, the hipster's oldest sister, apparently; smelly, gross, dirty dude: he basically was homeless and a junkie for heroin and coke and meth that he could get his hands on because he said it gave him 'peace in life,' as he put it, the way a woman gives birth to a child they see for the very first time and immediately adores beyond all reason, or the way the sun rises behind clouds in the Autumn sky, or the way you can simultaneously be eating bomb-ass spaghetti whilst your slut girlfriend is giving you the best blow-jobbie of your life, he said—and I laughed at), and we all three even talked about how we ended up at the hospital. Hipster said he had been there two weeks and wanted to go home, but that he got there because he had a fight with his parents about rent that made him go ballistic— a knife was involved in his story. Homeless said he just wanted three-hots-and-a-cot for a week, so he purposefully provoked a fight with a Palm Springs police officer whilst repeatedly claiming to be 'the son of God.' I told them I had a panic attack, and they proceeded to laugh at my face.

"These guys showed me to their room they were bunking together in. Homeless and Hipster were basically guitarists/ songwriters and had piles and piles of lyrics they said they came up with while they were here. They said that they didn't really remember sleeping there much, that all they did was drink the hospital's cheap coffee to stay motivated. I didn't disclose that I was a slightly somewhat successful writer because I didn't want to bring unwanted attention to myself in this dump. We all hung-out for hours and it was fantastic.

"A guy came into the room and said I had a visitor. It was my mother. He brought me into some visiting room. My mother came with a book called *The Financial Lives of the Poets* by Jess Walter. I had been talking about it a week prior and she had remembered I did and decided that day to get me it to lift my spirits. Optimism, obviously. I hugged her. Then this welfare lady came in and was talking about my future, saying that in order to pay this bill I inevitably would get I needed a proper source of income. My mother explained that I got to Florida just recently to get better mental health-wise before going on to pursue work, and it would take quite some time before we could even consider the option of payment to their high-income hospital. The lady understood and suggested that I get a low-key job, like being a sales clerk or stock-boy, or one of those guys at the toll-booths who take people's money, press a gate button, and hand them tickets all day for minimum wage. She said I would be successful at that, and immediately a sickness came over me at the pit of my stomach.

"After my mother left, I went to my room and stayed there reading Jess Walter's book. It was lovely and skillful; I was thoroughly jealous of his work. I got inspired and was pacing back and forth while writing on some napkins. Poetry, mostly. All of it was thrown in the garbage, but it felt good to get it down anyway. And just then, as I was doing this, this naked black kid with cross-eyes came into my room, the door wide open behind him (fortunately), and he was standing there, looking at me and masturbating aggressively. He didn't have the look of lust or sexual arousal though; he had the look of a sick man who had no idea where he was or what he was doing. He stepped forward, still looking at me and masturbating, and he said, 'The flat earth is all anyone knows to be t-t-*true!* We all float up here! We all are one with Satan!' A guy came in, who was obviously part of the hospital staff, while this weirdo was saying all this shit, and he told him, 'That's enough! Get your ass in solitary!' The weirdo was screaming, 'No! Nightmares! Drugs! No!' The guy grabbed hold of him, yanked him out of my room, and shut my door. I just shook my head.

"After a quick shower, I ate dinner and then we started playing board games and trivia. Even masturbating weirdo ended up playing. We all had a grand ole time and nobody seemed crazy at all. It all seemed as if it was elementary school again, and we just were embracing the heat of the moment, the pure joy of just being ourselves and laughing about nonsense and carrying on, a rare moment that happens maybe once a year to me, personally. It was nice and freeing, and for a second, I had no care in the world and almost no anxiety or depression. That night I slept great—or as great as I could, sleeping in a hospital where potentially anyone can walk in masturbating next to you.

"I stayed for two more days and kept to myself. That last day I was to do another 15-minute session with a doctor-lady. She was old, not hot, but approachable. I basically told her that I didn't think I had anything wrong with me, that I had a theory that what I was experiencing was depersonalization with glimmers of a single existential crisis on an hourly basis. I told her my examples of this and she concluded that I was right. She even created paperwork showing this. She said I was free to go. I waited hours before they finally discharged me. My mother took awhile to get to the hospital, but when she did, oh man, I was so happy I almost did a cartwheel. When I got home, my mom's dog Bella was very happy to see me. I picked her up and she was licking my ears she was so happy to see me. I cried so hard and I had no idea why.

"Honestly, the only reason I'm telling you this, Scott, is because I never told anyone about it. People think I'm some bitter, no-good, punk asshole, but really I'm a closet sweetheart. After that visit, I got a bill in the mail for about 2 grand. Obviously I didn't pay it because it was an awful stay. My mother even told me it was pointless. We went to another doctor who did blood work and a genetic swab thing on me. Turns out I had some vitamin deficiency and he prescribed me some vitamin and some Prozac to calm my head down, which he gradually increased with every future visit I had with him. It was the max dose he could give me, and I got better. My anxiety was gone. My depression was gone. I only follow my mood with whatever life gives me. Bad days have a bad mood, good days have good moods. That's the closest to normalcy I'll ever reach. And as I was in this state and felt alive, I became a very happy, healthy, nihilistic, atheistic troll who is sadistic, yes —but did all of it oddly with a sense of comedy and flattery that people enjoyed. I made more friends. I got better jobs. I saved. I got a car. I moved out. I got my own place. I did my own thing. Now I'm just waiting and watching my life pass by, and you know what, I'm okay with that, Scott."

Scott looks at you as if he's looking at someone he idolizes. His eyes and stature are relaxed, comfortable, and at ease. He says, "Thanks for telling me your story, Steve. I think you're my new best bud. Let's exchange numbers." Totally, you say, and you both make it happen. "Your story was hella long, though. It's almost dark. I had, like, 5 beers in the time it took you to explain all that shit. Let's cut the serious, depress-ful"—did he even say a correct *word?* you think—"shit and go to O'Shea's."

"Love that place," you say. "Let's do it."

"Let me close my tab."

"Me too."

While all the guys around this hot bartender chick probably gave her a fruitful tip, you decide not to tip her at all, not to give in to the exploits of her bodily assets that you know you would happily submit to. Scott tipped 25%, though, the lame-O. Everyone treats her like gold, you think. You reason that the best thing for her is to realize that she isn't as valued as everyone thinks or perceives her to be, that she isn't praised and valued by every male on the planet, that she is equal to the ugly chick bumming for money down the street-corner on a hot, sunny, Florida afternoon, or the hot supermodel in Los Angeles who has millions of followers on social media.

fourteen

You and Scott Geller are making your way downtown, walking fast, faces pass, and you're O'Shea's-bound—doo-doo doo doo-doo doo *doo!* It's pretty much nighttime, about the time nobody actually comes out but the party is just getting started, the strangely, oddly ominous time when that realm of dinner-time is somewhat turned magically into night-life, and everyone is either happy or pretending to be happy by being masked with copious amounts of alcohol and drugs. Scott tells you that he wants to avoid drinking too excessively because he exclusively tends to crave Cocaine when he's in that state of mind. He says he hasn't gotten sloshed in some time, though, so he doesn't plan for it to happen, but nevertheless, he comments about it anyhow.

And you and him make it to the entrance of O'Shea's. It's an Irish Pub that you've been to hundreds of times when taking out drunk chicks that you met either *at* O'Shea's itself, or at Hubbaloo next door. Or literally any bar, any place, anywhere else. The door is big, bulky, wooden, almost dungeon-like. Lights dim. A few business guys in there. A band is setting up. You recognize the singer: she's this chick from Tennessee traveling state-to-state, she says; but you think she's entirely full of shit because you've seen her play here dozens of times. They all play good music, though—mostly covers of Stevie Nicks and other oldies. But anyways, there's also framed pictures of things like fishing and cities on the walls. It vaguely has a green hue inside the entire place. There are a couple pool tables and, next to them, a display of stacked shirts whose frontal designs are rolled and folded in such a way that spells out "O'Shea's Irish Pub." Fantastic.

You and Scott sit down at the main bar, the stools fairly high, and you think for a moment what makes a bar cool—is it atmosphere? drink choices? women who frolic? the music playing? if smoking or non-smoking? the youth or old? To you, it seems to be all entirely the same, O'Shea's or Copper Blues. It's a feeling, though, that you and possibly Scott can't shake: the idea of "cool." The idea of "comfortable." The idea of what the bar brings you to, that moment of a "good-time" we all seek. This, to you, is Scott's place.

"I don't really like O'Shea's too much," he says.

Never mind, you think.

And he explains, "I mean, I like this 2-dollar mystery beer special they got going, but every time I do it I always end up with some shitty apple cider."

You say, "I always get IPAs. I don't really like IPAs, but it gets you drunk."

"So does apple cider . . . But you want to not look and feel like a ladyboy when you get to that point. Ah, fuck it! I'll just go for the cheapest to get drunk by. Mystery beers it is."

Tender comes up. "Hey. What's up?"

Scott says, "Nothing, man. Two mystery beers."

Tender nods. He comes back with two beers in brown bags. Scott hands him a 5-spot. The tender walks away.

"Ready for the reveal?" you say to Scott.

"Always am."

You both roll down the brown paper of your beer cans.

"Hell yeah!" Scott says. "Got an IPA!"

Laughing, you say, "I got a fuckin' Angry Orchard."

"That sucks, bro."

"Apple cider. Fuck my life."

"Oh well." Scott lifts his beer and says, "John Galt."

You cheers, kick back and drink.

After a few moments, you say, "You like Ayn Rand, don't you?"

"What, you don't?"

"I do! But not, like, quoting her all the time."

"I think she's amazing in every way. *Atlas Shrugged* is the best book ever."

"I think so, too."

"Who was your favorite?"

"Francisco d'Anconia."

"I like Rearden and Dagny."

"I think they're all great."

Suddenly, a chick passes by, bumping slightly into Scott's shoulder. She says, laughing, "My bad." Scott says, "It's cool, bro." She walks off. The both of you stare at her fat ass—it's phenomenal-looking. Scott turns back around and says to you, "Dammit, man. Women are addiction. Like heroin. Opium."

You nod.

"I'm serious when I say that, Steve."

You say, "I know you are."

"That reminds me."

"What?"

"Francisco d'Anconia's thing he says to Rearden towards the middle of *Atlas Shrugged*. Remember?"

"It's hazy."

"He pretty much tells Rearden a speech about how you can

tell about a man's self-esteem simply by the women he chooses."

"I remember that, yeah. I thought it was true."

"It is. Like us, we probably are total scumbags for chicks. We only look to build our self-esteem through the act of sex— or the pursuit of sex. It's meaningless, bro. It's not worth the effort because the sex doesn't fill that void. The sex is a means to an end. Francisco said that if he could see what woman a guy would pick he can tell you the guy's entire philosophy on life. It's just wild to me."

"What does this have to do with us . . . or anything for that matter?"

"That chick. Did you notice how trashy she looked?"

"I don't know, man. She looked pretty hot to me. I'd fuck her."

"That's just it! You'd fuck her. Why?"

"Honestly, because she looks like she has a perfect hole. I can just use it for my own selfish needs."

Scott laughs. "That's so trippy to me that Ayn Rand is right about this shit."

"What?" you say. "Tell me."

"You and I hate ourselves to the point where we want to fuck any woman decent enough to be pleasing in front of our faces, but ultimately her vag is the pump that takes care of our shitty needs, bro. However, I catch feelings easily, so I'm different."

"Yeah. Basically. But, uh, did you not like her?"

"What? The chick?"

"Yeah."

"Fuck yeah I did! I would lick her baby-cannon until she was squirming. She was hot! But I don't typically go for trashy. I kind of like just really cool, chill chicks that are just down. I don't know."

"I absolutely love trashy," you admit. "The trashier, the better. I loved that she was walking around as if everyone was watching. I love that her ass was bouncing around for me to see. It's the idea that she flaunts herself and me wanting to tear it up, almost to show to her and potentially any person who knows her that I had that."

"Anyone who knows her?"

"I don't know, man. When I fuck chicks, I always just hammer myself into them as hard as I can. I like to hear their reactions."

"Like screaming?"

"I mean, not like screaming *in pain*—more like screaming in pure ecstasy. If a chick is in pain from my cock, I would— Um, actually . . ."

"What?"

"It would turn me on. I like those pornos of black dudes with huge cocks fucking petite white chicks and how they freak-out about the size of their cocks." You laugh. "It's weird but true. I like the idea of them just being unsure to do it, but they do it anyway. I don't know. The regret in the middle of it is kind of hot, but they know they can't stop because, deep down, they like it and know they are just putting on a show."

"Like being fake?"

"Exactly like being fake."

"That's pretty much exactly how chicks are. But what if she isn't faking? What if she really is hurting but is just not saying anything to you? Maybe out of fear or shame or embarrassment. Maybe she doesn't want to upset you and make you feel like she's lame for not doing it. Like the very pressure of it all just overwhelms her and she takes the pain somehow away. This large object buried inside her vag. Like, this . . . *thing*. This thing that she hears her friends talk about how awesome it is but really it kind of hurts her. Maybe she dates you after because she feels confused about her feelings towards you because the very act feels like some justification of love. Maybe it's all a scam to her, the idea of men. Maybe you fuck her over and it makes every man that ever knows her after you get the burden of putting her broken pieces back together. Maybe she's just a person who wants to feel loved, and by you fucking her like that, maybe she gets corrupted in some sick, twisted way, doing sex acts in ways that, in actuality, she never wanted to perform ever in the first place."

You stare at Scott; Scott stares at you. It's silent for a moment. You grin; Scott grins. And then both your heads get thrown back, howling in brutal, unstoppable, gut-wrenching laughter. You hold your beers and almost spill them, you laugh so hard.

"Gay," you jokingly say.

Scott says, "My bad, bro. Who is John Galt?"

"I'll drink to that."

You both take long hits.

After chugging it all, you say, "But I'm still not into hurting chicks in bed. I think if it actually came time in the bedroom and the chick wasn't actually into it, I would stop or slow down or see if she was down to continue. I just would feel bad. Sex is not fun to me when the girl is not having fun too. Half the fun is not just getting my rocks off; half the fun is making *her* rocks get off, too—and making *her* have that look of satisfaction. It's empowering to satisfy a woman in bed. Plus it makes her want more and turns her into the biggest slut–whore imaginable. She'll do stuff willingly. Kinky shit. She'll do it because she truly is into you sexually and wants to please you. That's the sex I want. If a chick looks uncomfortable, I'll lose my wood. Straight up." Another beer comes randomly in front of you.

Scott says, "But you just said you like watching porn where the chick is in pain from cock."

You sigh. "Listen. Porn is fantasy. Porn is absolutely 100% bullshit. It's not meant to be real, it's meant to be taboo and naughty. You literally watch porn to see things you can't normally see, no matter how good you are at pulling chicks or how much you love your wife or girlfriend, seeing a whore with *huge*, huge tits fuck cock the way they do is just something you oddly want to watch, despite convictions of positivity towards women that a guy may or may not have. The kind of porn a man watches has nothing to do with the man himself and how he views women. It's simply just a means to get his rocks off in the meantime, when his girl is gone. But it is fun to watch cool or weird shit."

"I feel you."

"Yeah," you sigh, taking the last sip of your surprise beer.

"Another?" Scott says.

"Sure."

"Good. Next round is on you, bro."

"Hokay."

You wave the Tender over, he comes, does his thing, and you get two mystery beers again. This time you and Scott roll the brown bags down and reveal that you both have IPAs. Though you both should be hyped, for some weird reason you don't even comment on it, don't even have a care in the world. You crack them open and drink silently for a few moments together. . . .

Until Scott says, "Something is bothering me, Steve."

"What?"

"That chick."

"Which one."

"The trashy one."

"What about her?"

"I don't know. But I get the feeling she bumped into me purposely."

You look at Scott for a moment. It dawns on you frighteningly. "Yeah," you say. "Did she . . . ?"

"That's what I'm saying, bro. Like I wonder if she purposely bumped into us just to make us talk and think about it, just so she can have in her mind that she influenced us in some way."

"She did."

"I know she did."

"But I don't think she really cares."

"She does if it gets her rocks off, Steve."

You look down at your can. You twirl your finger around the outside, where the condensation is, and you spell out the word: "Real." You say to Scott, "I just don't think she cares because she doesn't gain anything from it. Sure, emotion."

"Gratification."

"Self-indulgence."

"Self-esteem."

"Pity."

"Hope."

You're shocked on that last one. "Hope?" you question. "Why hope?"

"I don't know, dude . . ." Scott takes a sip of his beer. "Just forget it. She was a cool thing to do. She was just a memory, a conversation, a fantasy, a drug, an addiction for us at this moment. She was meant for us to forget about the bullshit in our lives and to focus on something other than ourselves. We are all selfish, yes—but it's not that simple."

You ask, "Why did you say 'dude' just now?"

"What?" Scott squints. "What do you mean?"

"You always say 'bro,' not 'dude.' Why?"

Scott laughs. "Drink up, ladyboy. Stop overthinkin' shit." He holds up his can. "Just chill." You hold up yours. You both cheers. "Relax."

For the next moments—moments that change into seconds, minutes, hours, days, weeks, months, years, decades, centuries, millennias, infinities—you and Scott drink as many beers as you want: it's that moment where you're lost in a dream, a consciousness that fleetingly never falls behind the wheel of tomorrows, a will for change, for hate, for love. The will to be completely free and to understand yourself and your mind. To connect with others because you want so desperately to connect with yourself. You drink your beers and have no idea how many of them are passing through your system—and frankly, you don't even care to guess.

After these passing moments, after conversations of specific dynamics of life, after talking of love, baby-makers, and literally anything else that gives you or him pleasure—and laughing about it hysterically—you ask Scott, almost as an after-thought, "Yo. How many beers did we just drink, man?"

He smiles and says, "Never enough."

You frown.

And Scott says, "Chill. You had maybe, like, three beers."

You say, "Seems like more."

"You're weird, man. Don't be a ladyboy. I'm gonna go outside."

Scott stands and leaves. You watch him go. You wait. You look at your condensation-fogged can in front of you. For maybe a few minutes, you think of how much you don't know yourself. You write, through the condensation again, the word, "Hope," and stand up and walk outside with your hopeless can in hand.

fifteen

YOU'RE OUTSIDE O'SHEA'S.

Looking around to your right, you don't see Scott. You're wondering if he ran off somewhere and that you now have to find a drinking buddy to have fun with, though that usually isn't hard the more you drink alcohol and the more confidence you get.

Looking to your left, at the wooden table, you see Scott laughing with his head back, a couple in front of him: the chick is tall, beautiful, intimidating, red lipstick, almost "punky" in a way, and she appears to not be laughing—she looks like the kind of girl that would only laugh at something that is legit funny and not to impress anyone or anything other than to be genuine to herself, a feminist, a strong, independent woman; and the guy, well, the guy is tall too, long hair, goofy mustache on, a blue, biker-looking jacket on with a PBR patch stitched on the right front chest part. The both of them are drinking draft beer(s). It's piss yellow. You hope it's not something lame like Corona or something. You hate people that like Corona.

"Hey," you say to Scott when you walk up, interrupting the conversation at hand between the three of them.

"Oh, suh *dood!* This is . . ."

The dude of the couple says, in a very botched, very comedic Russian accent, "Randy the Russian! The *fuckin'* Russian to *you*, fag!" He points to his girlfriend. "And this is Batlana, Queen of the Bats!" and she says, "We don't know this guy. Shouldn't we give him our real names?"

Scott says, "Nah! I just met the guy. He's cool, though. His name's Steve." He turns to you. "Sit down, ladyboy!"

This is classic. You scoot in next to Scott's right. You wonder who these people in front of him are. Looking from left to right, at Batlana and Randy the Russian, you ask them how they know Scott.

Randy the Russian answers with: "I know Scott from a mutual writer friend of mine who I've known for a couple years now. But anyways, man, me and my friend know Scott because he works at this sub shop on F——— and M———. He hooks it up too."

Scott says, "Because you my boys!"

"Thanks, fag. So yeah, basically, um, that's how we know him. You guys just met?"

You say, "Yeah, we met over at Copper Blues."

"I fucking hate that faggy-ass place."

Batlana says, "You only hate it because the crowd is not people you're into."

"That's enough reason."

Batlana laughs at him.

Randy the Russian, now in a very "faggy," very feminine-sounding voice, says to her, "Listen, bitch! How 'bout you go down to Chili's, order the shitty 2-for-20 wit'cho broke ass, complain about it, get it for free, leave without tipping, then go to Burger King and get the 2-for-10, not getting bacon or cheese wit'cho broke ass . . . !"

Scott and Batlana bust out laughing; you begin to realize

that Mr. Randy the Russian is a clown, but an entertaining clown at that. He looks at you and says, almost as an additive to the joke, "You ole '*LOVE* that chicken from *Popeyes!*' lookin' ass!"

"You're wild," you say to him.

"Thanks, man. I'm thinking of doin' stand-up one of these days at Respectables. They do an open-mic every last Wednesday of the month."

Scott says, "I love the tail over at Respects."

Randy the Russian grins. "Whelp, I can't because"—he points at Batlana—"this one over here won't allow it."

Batlana says, "You're damn right!"

Randy the Russian laughs and says, "Yo guys, Bonnie is fuckin' savage, yo"—you're guessing Batlana's real name is actually Bonnie—"because, listen, on her 30th birthday, we came down here to O'Shea's and Bonnie got trashed as fuck and there was this chick outside whose ass got slapped by some drunk asshole. Anyways, the chick was bitching about it. We crossed the street for some shit, came back, and the chick was there. Out in the middle of the road, Bonnie was telling this chick about herself and—"

Interrupting him, Bonnie says, "Yeah! I asked her basically how old she thought I was and she was like, 'Uh, you look about 30.' I almost slapped a bitch over that shit."

Randy the Russian starts laughing. "She was like, 'Listen, bitch, lemme get your number so we can meet up for a peti, because, bitch, your toes look BUSTED!"

Bonnie starts giggling. Scott and you howl with laughter. Randy the Russian continues, in the "faggy" voice again, "Bitch! You look like when the cops in Grand Theft Auto catch you and the screen says"—he motions the air in front of him with his hand—"the word 'BUSTED' in the middle!"

Scott says, "You are"—he's crying he's laughing so hard —"such a fuckin' ladyboy!"

"Fuck you, fatty, limp-dick fuckboy!"

"Love you!"

"Yeah, yeah, yeah"—takes a sip—"love you too, faggot."

Bonnie says, "You know Brandon starts a new job?"

You're guessing Randy the Russian's name is actually Brandon.

Scott says to him, "Yeah, man. Congrats."

"Thanks. 4-days a week, 10-hour shifts, biiiiiiiitch! Was*suh!*"

"Sounds gravy."

You ask Brandon, "Where do you work?"

"This meat place. Pays good, seems simple. I'm a chef."

"Oh," you say, laughing, "like Gordon Ramsey?"

Brandon grins. "Gordon Ramsey is my fuckin' nigga!" He slaps his hand on the table, twists his palm, picks up, with his index and thumb, an invisible piece of a burger patty or something. He says, in a British accent or some shit, "The fuck is this?! Well done, bloke! Looks like *Gondi's* fuckin' flip-flop!" Everyone is laughing. He says, "Looks like something Tiger Woods would tee off with!"

You say, "That dude, man. So funny."

Brandon says, "My last job I felt exactly like that dude. Just an angry piece-of-shit. I was the best person there, and I knew it. My buddy, the other writer I told you about, he started there months after I got there. Didn't know shit about cooking, man. Two months in, he was better than this drunk asshole I work with who claims to have been through years of culinary school."

You ask further, "Drunk asshole?"

"Yeah!" Brandon almost glares at you in a deep, stern, serious manner. "This guy—I don't want to say his name—he would come in clearly drunk, bitching, bitching, bitching. Always bitching about *some*thing. 'Safety, guys! Start saying you're be*hind* me!' And he would just constantly do shit that was blatantly annoying. That writer buddy told me that one morning he was opening the restaurant with this other cook. It was a hotel we all worked at. Anyways, my buddy and this other cook didn't turn on the oven because, to be honest, breakfast you don't really need the oven. And when lunch comes around, if it's dead and nobody orders, like, a pizza or some shit, then I'm sorry, the oven is not fucking needed. This drunk fuck came in towards the end of lunch, opened the oven because the red light wasn't on, and he goes, 'Yo! Oven not on!' and he goes, 'See?' and he reaches inside the obviously cold oven and starts banging the rack, making noises 'n' shit."

Scott says, "Yeah, fuck that."

"I know. And one day"—Brandon is looking at you—"my writer buddy and I were working. He worked open; I was a mid-shift. So he was gonna leave and I had to work with this drunk fuckboy chef. So I was making a joke with the servers and bartenders back in the kitchen because it was pretty slow. I go to the 86 board and I'm like, 'Hey, everyone! Let's start putting our bets in on how much beer fuckboy drank before work!' Everyone knew who I was talkin' about. One yelled '8!' One yelled '12!' One yelled '20!' One yelled '3' and also '0.' I wrote them down with letters next to the numbers. That's it. Anyways, the guy came in, reeking of booze, and I was laughing with the guy, talking about drinking beer and smoking weed. He said he had some before work, and he was laughing about it. So I asked him how many beers he had. I shit you not, he told me he had 6. *And* he had like half a bottle of bourbon, he said. So we all fuckin' lost the bet. I told him about the bet, like, you know, as a fucking *joke*, and I brought him to the 86 board. He was laughing about it or whatever and we all thought nothing of it. I left the kitchen to go smoke a cigarette. My buddy told me that this fuckboy was angry, telling him how 'unprofessional' it is that we made bets like that on him. He took photos of the 86 board on his phone and even said, 'Yeah, it is funny, but *very* unprofessional.' He stormed out of the kitchen apparently, went to H-fuckin'-R, and told on me. They investigated, I got written-up and bitched at, and little do they know they defended a fucking drunk fuckboy. Everyone—the servers, managers, bartenders—they all lied and said that the real bet on the 86 board was for 'how many specials we would sell.' Everyone lied. And he still got me bitched out about it. That was when I knew how gay the guy was. So you know what I did?"

You ask, "What did you do?"

And Brandon smiles. "I did nothing. Every single shift, I refused to speak to him. He would go out of his way, even in front of managers to try and make me speak, and I refused. The managers would tell me it's not professional to do that to a coworker. I laughed and told them, 'Yeah, well, it's not fucking professional to drink before work, admit it, and then blame a guy who is busting his balls and gets him into trouble with HR. So fuck him.' And I said it just like that, those assholes. And you know what? They just smiled because they knew they hated him too. We had a theory that this fuckboy had dirt on the GM and therefore was immune to being let go. I even asked that, they just smiled about it, like I was joking or some shit. And this guy still did the same shit, drinking and bitching, bitching and drinking. I got tired of it. Even one of my managers got tired of it. He was paid like shit like all of us, put in his two-weeks, found another job, whatever. Then they hire a fucking sous chef, even though, the fucktard's logic, there is no fucking *head* chef! Like, who are you assisting, bro?!"

You say, "Fuck, that's so shit." Bonnie and Scott aren't listening, as if they already know the story. They're talking about a comedy show or something.

Brandon continues: "This sous chef is 24 years old, dumb as fucking rocks, like 400-pounds, so he's taking up space and is in the way of the line, and he claimed, I shit you not, on his resumé, that he was The Rock's personal fucking chef. And yeah, so, I researched The Rock's diet and—"

You say, "Wait. Dwayne 'The Rock' Johnson?"

"Correct. This sous chef says he was his 'personal chef.' So I did research and apparently, The Rock eats a diet of chicken and, like, maybe two starches and like very lean meals, all the same, 6-times a day. No way in fuck this 400-pound, 24-year-old fuckboy got a job like that, worked alone in his kitchen, and was making that shit for him. The guy would Google literally everything before he would do anything in the kitchen. He was lying. And they hired him, the first guy that applied. I'm literally thinking this whole time that if I just waited a couple months and waited for his sous chef position and got it myself, I would be paid his $20 an hour. I was paid $12. And this dude was my fucking *boss!* How shit is that? Able to bark orders and shit, not doing a damn thing but pretending to do work. Then you got fucking servers and shit, impatient and don't know how to work the computers for orders and tickets, making 4-times the amount of money I was in a single—" Brandon shakes his head. "Wait? *Why* am I talking about this shit? Fuck that place. Good riddance. I'm about to start a better job and be happier, hopefully. Fuck that, man." He raises his beer. "Cheers, bro." You cheers him. "I like you, man," he says, taking a sip. "You're sick."

"Thanks, man," you nod.

"What are you into?"

"Huh?"

"Like, you know, I play metal and shit—so what do *you* do?"

"I don't know." You think for a moment. "I just like pussy."

Bonnie, striking her conversation with Scott to a sudden halt, says, "What?"

You say, "Uh, I really just want to get laid. That's all I'm into."

She stares at you intently, disturbed. "So let me get this straight: you don't know us, we're outside of a bar, and my boyfriend says he cooks and makes music, and you pop off with saying that you like pussy?"

You shrug. "I guess so. It's just playful."

"Do you not find anything wrong with this picture?"

Brandon and Scott are talking now, not paying any attention to you or Bonnie's conversation. They are talking about how a hipster kid walking by has "boat shoes" on, and how he probably doesn't even own a boat or ever even cares to —probably the hipster is following a trend of some sort, "like a faggot does," Brandon adds as an after-thought, laughing.

Bonnie says to you, not wanting to hear an answer from you, "The kind of guys like you, the kind of guys that go around just getting girls and 'playfully,' as you claim, coercing them into sex, into a fake feeling, into a fake-ass love of some sort, are the kind of guys that should be castrated. You should be ashamed of yourself. Let me guess, you go around saying anything and everything that these women, these powerful, strong, independent, intelligent women, want to hear; you will do anything and everything to get into their pants and make them gain a false sense of happiness; you'll bring them down to your level of self-hatred and use them and abuse them for your own selfish bidding because *you're* the asshole, not them —they 100% did nothing wrong to you. They are beautiful. They are amazing. We are the best. I consider myself a feminist, yes—but not the stereotypical, I-hate-every-creature-with-a-penis kind of way, no—I just want women to be shown respect. And by you saying shit like, 'I just, uh' "—she impersonates your retarded face she views you as—" 'kind of, like, want *pussy*, I guess,' it makes me livid and completely is the reason why women are feminists in the first place. Women aren't here to be your piece of shit-meat that you fuck, day-in, day-out. We're here to live just like you're here to live. I just had to say that to your ass. My bad."

You sigh, "No, it's my bad. I should've known better."

Bonnie sighs too but in a relieved sort of way. "It's okay, man. Just be considerate. Stop being a dick and saying shit like you 'wanting some pussy.' I'm sure you preach it all the time or else you wouldn't have popped off with that bullshit to people you barely know. Just chill! Live life and have fun! Drink! Jump, run, laugh! Do anything you want and don't be a busted-ass faggot."

You nod. "Thanks, Batlana."

"Call me 'Bonnie.' " She smiles.

"I'm a closet sweetheart, I swear."

"I'm sure you are, but you gotta show it."

"I get you." And you really do.

Brandon says, as if he and Scott have a fantastic idea, "Yo, let's go to Respects."

Bonnie's eyes light up. "Yeah! I want to get my damn dance on!"

Brandon shakes his head. "Women . . . All the same."

Bonnie gives him a flirt punch. Afterward, he pulls her in, says, "Baby, I la' you," and gives her a kiss. Clearly she looks embarrassed, as if she isn't comfortable with affection in public, but she allows it because you bet it was a reaction in his brain, a reaction of a feeling that you wish you could feel for another human being, could give your all to, selflessly, and make them warm inside.

Scott says, "You guys are cute together. . . ."

You all three stand up, go inside O'Shea's, pay your tabs, talk about how lame some "trashy chick" at the bar is (Bonnie says), talk about how he used to go here during his work shifts and down shots (Brandon says), talk about how he really wants Cocaine (Scott says), and you all four walk out of this bar and cross the damn street, Respectables-bound.

sixteen

DRUNK, YOUNG, AND DUMB, you're crossing the street realizing that all three things have suddenly become a reality, a moment that, oddly, has never dawned on you; you're just a simple man doing simple things in his simple town-life; a man who, despite thinking, feeling, and assuming that he knows himself completely, has no idea what he is doing with his life or what he has ever wanted to do. It's just about having that good ol'-fashion dopamine intake in the brain that you naturally have the unfortunate trouble with producing.

You all four make it to the entrance of Respectables. Brandon gives the guy dap, the guy nods, and you all don't have to pay the measly 5-dollar entry fee. You go on it. No smoke, some lights, it's dim . . . Couches line the walls, super comfy, no tables, as if it's there for resting after a long night of dancing, as if they are there to serve you and the woman you so choose—and she choosing you back, of course—the woman you pull a seat with, make-out with, dance again maybe, buy beers, and hopefully bring to either your place or her place and do the lovely golden deed. The couches serve well. You all four walk towards the bar. Bonnie says, "It's packed tonight."

At the bar, Brandon asks for a PBR and, in fact, quadruples the order, telling the bar-bitch to get them for him and you three. He's feeling generous, you think, as most do when the alcohol fills your system with eager hospitality. The bar-bitch smiles, nods, and promptly comes back with 4 beers, opening them all in front of you four. Brandon leaves a 20 down. Bonnie actually hugs the bar-bitch from behind the counter. Bonnie says to her, "How are you?!" "Good!" "You still having to deal with that asshole?" "Nah, fuck him. Just been working, that's all." "I need a massage, bitch. You still doing them?" "Duh, bitch!" "We'll talk." "Ditto." Bonnie and her hug once more. Brandon turns to you and says, "You should hit that, faggot."

Scott, leading your group to the back outside of the club, is chugging his beer before he even has time to bump into someone, anyone, and say sorrys or my-bads or anything to some Boynton Beach ghetto asshole-fuck clown-boy who is trying to get a simple whore to dance with him. Scott runs into one, they nod, and it's not the least bit critical. Scott throws the can. Brandon is laughing his ass off. Bonnie isn't paying much attention. They have Outkast's hit song "Roses" playing over the speakers; she's singing along and dancing whilst following behind Brandon. Scott gets to the middle of the outside courtyard-y thingamajig and sees some long-haired hipster guy. Scott yells, "Pete! Hey, asshole! How you been?!" The hipster guy turns around excitedly and says, "Scott! My nigga! I'm doing good!" "How's that one chick doing?" "My girlfriend?" "Yeah!" "She and I broke up." "Whatever. Yo, do you got . . ." "Nah, Scotty-boy. I don't sell that shit anymore." "Come on!" "My buddy with me does, though. Here." The guy pulls Scott along and they both disappear between crowded, packed bodies.

You feel a tap on your shoulder. You spin around. There is a black kid looking at you; he says, "Holy shit. Steve!" and gives you a bear hug. "I haven't seen you since fuckin' *high* school, bruh!" You say to him, "Yeah, man. Help me out. Who are you?" "Damn, bruh. Fucked-up. I'm Trey, bro. Trey T——. You were in my American History class 'n' shit. You always would talk shit and correct the teacher 'n' shit. Would have the whole class *die* laughing! Ha-*ha!* Shit was classic, bruh!" "Yeah," you say, scratching your head. "Still don't remember. Sorry." "It's cool. You still skating?" "Huh?" "Skating!" "Nah, not really. I gave that shit up. I did everything I wanted to with it. Got boring for me." "What! You were killin' it, bruh! You would do crazy-ass ollies and kick-flips over the weirdest shit. I remember you ollie some rock-to-rock in some video I saw on YouTube or some shit. Fuckin' wild, bruh!" "Yeah. Those days are gone. I did everything I wanted to." "Setting the bar low, don't you think?" You stare at him; you answer with, "The goals I make are mine and only mine, and if I achieve them, I simply move to a bigger and better goal. Setting my bar high in high school is what I did with the sponsors, the videos, the status, everything. I achieved great shit doing what I loved. So I'm cool with it."

A white chick, 22-ish, hot, wearing ripped, tight jeans, a "Fucking Awesome" shirt, red boat shoes, and a weird-looking Breast Cancer Awareness bracelet, comes walking up behind Trey, looks at him, says, "What's up, babe?" then at you, stops everything she's doing—hanging-out, dancing, drinking, having a good, grand ol' time, literally anything—and her eyes get wide as she says, out loud, "Holy shit!" She bows. "Steven!" She stands back upright and then gives you a hug, just like Trey did. "You're fuckin' Steven! You were a killer on a skateboard!" You smile for a second, not because of the compliment, not because of her being beautiful and complimenting, not because you want to fake an enjoyment of the situation of admirers and their recollections of your past accomplishments. It's because you have the swift, vaguely distant memory that flushes into your psyche of a time when you actually *did* have admirers, actually *did* have people who respected you to some extent, actually *did* have some inch of value in the lives of others. It's this smile and feeling that add to your spark of confidence as you say to this chick standing next to her black boyfriend who you don't remember much of, "Yup, I'm Steve! *That guy!*" "I remember you made those funny-ass videos back in the day." "Yeah?" "Yeah! You were fucking famous, bro!" "Thanks. You guys should buy me a beer." Trey butts in: "Nah, we actually gotta go. Nice seein' you, though." Trey puts his arm around the chick and she waves goodbye to you. They walk away. You don't even turn around; your smile vanishes as quickly as it came.

You look round and can't find Bonnie, Brandon, or even Scott, who he probably would try to find *you* guys. You stand on tippy-toes, looking off above the crowd. You see Brandon, laughing with his beer in the air, it spilling slightly, and it looks as though there is sweat on his arms, glistening and whatnot. You make way for him, shimmying passed everyone, bumping elbows, taking names, *beans, greens, potatoes, tomatoes* . . . You finally get to Brandon. You stand beside him. He's talking to some chick: "So you got your ass married now?! Holy shit! He's, like, cool as fuck I hear. How can he pull you, though? You're, like, not a total bitch," he turns to you, "Steve! Yo, buddy! This is a chick you should meet. She'll probably give you a handy or some shit." You look at her, she's smiling awkwardly with a wine glass in hand, with some weird concoction with a strawberry or something with a stem drooped over the side, one end floating there, soup-like. What is strange is that you know Respects does not serve wine, so you vaguely assume that maybe she snuck it in? You don't know. You try not to look at it because it almost disgusts you. You say to her, "Suh, girl." "Hey!" "You married?" "Yeah, just got married two weeks ago." "That sucks." "Why's that? This outta be good." "Because now you only have one cock to suck." "Excuse me?" "Yeah. One cock." "I love my husband." She gives you a quick, non-brutal slap on the face. She says, "How fuckin' *dare* you!" You wipe your cheek and smile. "Feisty. You must be the *queen* in bed!" Brandon is laughing his ass off. The chick says, "You fuckin' suck!" and Brandon says to you, "Smoooooooooth . . ."

Bonnie comes walking up, she says hi to the chick, knows her, gives her a hug, they briefly talk about her new marriage, the wedding, how awesome it was, if the honeymoon was good, giggles and whatever, girl-talk. Afterward, Bonnie says to her, "We are gonna dance, Brandon and I. Wanna join?" "Sure!" the chick says. She downs her drink. Brandon, Bonnie, and the chick all hold hands and go through the crowd like pros. You think for a moment of being the fourth wheel, a guy who can't even get the third-wheel chick to dance with you, that big of an outcast, a loser, a piece of shit. And just when you think further into it, Scott comes up to you all excited. He's in your face: "Bro! I scored *this!*" He holds up an 8-ball. "Let's get fuckin' LIT!" He opens the baggie a little, grabs a house key out of his front pocket, dips the key inside the bag, pulls out, does the bump right in front of everyone (nobody even seems to look or care), and then he hands you the key and baggie, saying, "Do it. It's good shit. Proper blow, ladyboy." You grab them, dip the key in, pull out, and, right before you snort, you think to yourself how you have never done Cocaine before (you think, but can't be sure entirely), how you have always maybe messed with alcohol or ole Mary Jane, how you were told this causes people with mental health problems to induce an unknown psychosis in their brains. You do it anyway, the hill, the white bohemian-powered hill, the big crystals of amusement. You draw in and it hits you like lightning. Your brain funnels inward, your nose feels electrified and numb, all at once. You feel excited in an instant, awake, wanting to do anything, wanting to take over the world. "This is, like . . ." You trail. "Holy shit." Scott says, "Let's dance with some sluts, ladyboy."

Inside the club, out on the dance floor, you're dancing with two hot, black, hipster hardbodies as they grind their asses and vulvas up and down you. You grab them aggressively. The lights explode in your eyes, it seems. Everything is vivid, serene, inviting, and golden. You can do anything. You grab both the chicks and start making-out with them, feeling their tiny flat chests (which you oddly don't get disappointed by), pulling them into you, wanting to be inside, wanting to feel every orifice of their hard bodies. You stop, look up: lights flash: green, blue, yellow, then white, a bright white, almost *too* bright, it hurts. You yell, "Fucking fuhhhhhhhhhhhhhh-*ck!*" and nobody can hear you, nobody even cares, you feel like this is the ultimate therapy, like being able to kill cats, kill humans, kill bees, kill planet Earth, screaming, with a bat, you grow bat wings, you grow horns, you fly, to Transylvania, to England, you see Emma Watson, Daniel Radcliffe, that red-headed fuckboy Ron, they are dressed in capes, they throw live dolphins, they yell and scream at you, they yell and scream at . . .

You feel dizzy. You look around, see nobody you know. The girls are dancing with someone else. You shrug but then see Scott and Brandon by the bar, hunched together. You run towards them, put your arms around them, and ask, "Suh?" Scott laughs. Brandon is doing a key-bump. He passes it to

Scott. Scott does one; he passes it to you. You do one. Same feelings, same result. You feel alive, on fire, and, strangely, a sense of hope. You don't want this feeling to go away. Scott and Brandon start going onto the dance-floor; they do their thing; they don't care about anything but enjoying this single moment, this one single, joyously blissful moment when you can do literally anything and no laws or social constructs exist, a moment exclusive to the night-life. The dizziness doesn't stop; you feel your head. You walk toward the walls, where couches are. Nobody is really at them, only one or two guys: one is yaking into a trashcan in front of him, the other, well, the other is completely passed the fuck out, slumping in his seat, wearing really nice clothes, new shirt, pants, probably new underwear, if you had to guess, very business-like shoes of some sort—names of brands you're bad with. Your brain is moving too fast. You sit down. You hold your head, looking off into the crowd of people dancing. You analyze the animals in this kingdom of hip-moving, ass-bending, and blatant intoxication. . . .

A girl—I'm sorry, a "woman"—probably 19 (but the guy in front pretended like she showed her I.D. and he gave her the green-green highlighter bracelet anyway to allow her entry, you imagine)—is dancing in front of two Spanish men. They're clearly smoking weed whilst she grinds up against them: you wonder what's going on through her mind. Is she thinking about her father, and how he's home, maybe drunk, maybe with his new wife (the chick's step-mother), and her being a super bitch to this girl because she wants her completely out of the picture. You think of the movie *The Parent Trap* and this makes you shake your head. No—too easy. She's the type that goes to a college, maybe even down the street, and these are the guys she met downtown, guys who probably lied to her about the kind of "good time" she will have with them, guys that will do and say anything to win her over. Not even for just sex, but just to have the look in her eyes, a look that you have seen before (coming from women), the look of mystifying persuasion, the look that only arises when you completely own them and cause them to be in a mindless trance. These men feed off that. This 19-year-old will one day (if she doesn't kill herself by drugs, stress, alcohol, depression, or a simple car accident) wake up and be 28, still hot but not as hot as she once was, still getting looks from men but older and older, she notices, as the years go by; and this chick will realize how many guys have played her and promised her the world and not delivered a single time, not even left her with a single thing to show for. She will look at married friends of hers and how happy they all are and realize that love is the answer, genuine, honest, wholehearted love from a man who feels the same way back; and she will sign up on Match-dot-com, eHarmony, literally any dating site where people have to pay because, ironically, people who pay for services tend to value them, she realizes. And she will find a man, forget about all these guys, these kinds of guys in front of her: low-life fuckboys, you think. She will forget them and live her life with a prideful man, have children, a home, everything under the sun, and she will beg and plead for her daughter (if she *has* a daughter, of course) to not go down the same path that she took—but obviously the daughter won't listen out of spite and the cycle continues. . . .

A fat kid—"man," I mean, sorry—is dancing with one really hot, really short, petite chick. She has a beer in hand. She looks like a winner, a chick who is nonjudgemental. But this fat guy, who can't even see his cock when he looks down to take a piss, feels a sense of wonder on how he managed to even get her to give him a chance on this dance-floor. He's a comedian, smart, everything she is looking for in a guy, but he feels scared; he feels scared he will fuck-up, and this is his downfall, his complete failure. She will end up being the one that got away. She will end up shaking her head at men who aren't confident enough in themselves as she is. She is perfection, and she knows it. Her hair in the morning, she spends hours on her hair to make it neat and presentable. Glasses, she has spent time in Glass World down in Palm Springs area and spent thousands on different looks of glasses just to look a way that is completely cute and irresistible to any human being—man or woman. She goes to any interview and nails it, especially if the interviewer is a guy, a guy who is a boss and wants to make money and knows that attractiveness is valued amidst customers in his establishment. This chick looks at this fat man and thinks that he is different because, in this moment, slightly docile, drunk, and "himself," he appears to show no sign of weakness. It's this night that marks the day in her mind, now and forever, that he is worth her time. You think about it and laugh because it bugs you out: the feeling of that hope in another human being.

Then you think of your old girlfriend, the one who cheated on you when you were sick in the head, and how much you missed that feeling of hope in another human being, how much it completed you, mystified you, entranced you, persuaded you of everything you've ever wanted and desired: the feeling of someone "loving" you. And you think, *Oh shit, I was duped! I was completely and utterly duped just like that chick with the two Spanish men,* but you're not the chick, no, your ex was the Spanish men, and you *allowed* yourself to be the chick. Your sickness, well, your sickness was the fat guy, there, depressed, unsure, alone, needing attention, needing hope, needing love, but it never comes because the insecurities—just like the fat guy—engulf you, overwhelm your entire being, your entire *existence*, and you cave inward and let the world crash before you, and your mental health diminishes greatly before your very eyes. You lose everything you've ever had, you hit rock-fucking-bottom. You cry some nights, wishing the memory of her will go away and stop torturing you into an endless void in the pit of your stomach. The only way that you imagine you can fill that endless void is with duping chicks, duping smart, innocent, lovely chicks and bringing them down to your shit level, making them feel the pain and making them cry, too. The feeling of blowing loads in women is not even the dopamine that happens in the brain—like you think, no—it's actually the very feeling of pulling a fast one on them, making them believe in you and believe in your integrity as another human being. It bothers you so bad because you were never this way prior to the heartbreak. You don't want to be that guy. You don't want to be that guy who stereotypically fucks people over just because you were fucked over, too, in the past, by the very type of women you continue to fuck over on Tinder, in bars, in grocery stores, in the DMV, online, literally anywhere. They catch on. 5 months. 5 months is all it takes for them to realize—sometimes unfortunately sooner. They don't want the scum of the earth like you around, killing their souls. They want the men that overcome this feeling, despite how much it kills them inside. They want the men that treat them perfectly, the way they were never treated. But you always feel sick with that feeling because the sick you feel, the hatred you feel, overwhelms you and it strangely gives you a sense of comfort to never leave that place in your mind and your emotions. You look out in this dance floor and see the fat guy, the chick in front of him, the 19-year-old chick, the two Spanish guys in front of her, and she and them all dancing, and they start kissing, maybe making-out (you can't tell the difference), and how much they don't care about these feelings you have. You envy that, get pissed, stand up, and dart out of Respectables, leaving behind everyone in this place.

seventeen

You're thinking . . . *I don't give a fuck about my life.* It's becoming that time when you supersede your old, hollowed, fragmented self and replace it with the bold, bright, thoroughly objective higher self—full of nihilistic depression that you have always known since the beginning of your existence but never have been completely conscious of. You walk westward down the left side of the street, looking at people passing: there's a couple, there are three groups of black men drinking and smoking, and walking passed is a red-dressed broad strutting on by as the black men cat-call her and she, surprisingly, obliges and has that look of coy bashfulness but the obviously hidden agenda of wanting them for the taking, the trade-off of the bad men, the men that give a rush she will never experience with any other, and the couple, just a few feet ahead, notices this, and the girl of the couple whispers something cruel in her man's ear: probably something hateful, jealous, rude, annoying, all the things to a man that are unpleasant, but he nevertheless listens and goes with it because he doesn't want to upset her, doesn't want to give any sense of an answer or opinion on the red-dressed broad, because he, too, would happily delve into her pants given the opportunity and the right conditions—namely, the condition of being dumped by his hateful girlfriend whispering obviously hateful things in his horny, manly ear. This is only a fraction of a second that you come to this judgmental conclusion of the people nearest to you, and you shake your head and wonder if it is at all accurate, or if you're just a bigot faggot trying to uncover the very nature of people who appear to look and feel and act happy whilst in the presence of literally anyone. Though you are unhappy, now crossing passed a lone bench, one that you have talked to friends at about chicks you couldn't score with on the belief that you didn't adequately press and execute the right attraction switches at the exact moment she desires, you think for a moment how scared you are, how little of a man you are, but then you think that that is majority opinion of happy-go-lucky ass-clowns that poison the world around you. You are a complete narcissistic, sociopathic fuckboy and that's who you will always be. You're tired of hiding it and pretending that you're something else, something that others want you to be, which causes this unhappiness to fester and thrive in the first place. You think of how genuine you are to feel this pain and sadness, despite not wanting or needing it to occur, the unpleasant reality hitting headfirst into your psyche. It's a genuine tone on your mind. A bum is sitting at a table next to a group of probably friends laughing with their heads back about some trivial television show or the way someone looks when they are drunk and miserable. The bum sitting there, staring at these groups of people, shouting profane things at the top of his lungs, and everyone looking over and laughing at him. Is he genuine? You pass him and he says to you, "The world is fucking ending! The world is a fucking pigsty!" and you say, smiling proudly, "Don't you and *I* know it." You high-five each other and, in this moment, there's a spark in this bum's eye of feeling a sense that he is not crazy, that his drinking is justified, that he isn't the biggest piece of shit the world over. He smiles and it's the one smile you can level with in some fucked-up way. It's the smile of something genuine. He points over at some statue that rests on the other side of the crosswalk you are obviously about to cross, heading southbound towards your residence. The bum shouts, "I climbed that sum'bitch!" You believe him. You believe him because when you were in high school you too climbed it and got to the top and looked on out into the street and even at the police station across the street from it. You flicked off the cops that weren't there—nowhere to be found. Probably they were fighting crime off somewhere on Tamron and not enforcing the law on lowlifes climbing artistic architecture. You remember this and smile, not looking back at this bum that you want to forget about entirely because he has no value in your life. Your phone is vibrating but you don't even want to look at it or even consider talking to another human being, even as some walk past you as if you are just another drunk guy that they have seen a million times before when out with their friends. Your phone is a sickness. The women are both a sickness and an addiction. You start running and eventually you pass this building. . . . It's not even a building, per se, it's more of a house made to wed people at. You remember a time when you were talking to this chick who had a boyfriend of 3 or so years, she said—at the time (and this was when you were a virgin still)—and how even though she openly admitted that she did in fact like you romantically and wanted so badly to kiss you and teach you to not be afraid of the women around you, she still invited you to this house you're looking at whilst running for no apparent reason. It was her wedding to this guy she loved. She invited you to take photos of it and even dance with her best friend who was invited, too. The friend was a redhead, beautiful, sassy, and fun to her core; she and you danced at one point, looked into each other's eyes and had that singular look of a desire to kiss, but you simply stopped, looked away, and rested your head on her shoulder, avoiding the kiss altogether, knowing damn good and well how much of a royal pussy you are for not making the move that she wanted you, the man, to make. You watched your friend get married and you took photos of it all, depressed while you did it because you wished you were in that position—not with *her* specifically but with the girl of your dreams in general. Marriage is dead. Marriage doesn't last long. But strangely this chick, last you checked, is still married to her guy and they are happy as clams—no children, either. You shake your head and try to erase those memories from your mind as you pass the Publix you saw Bill at. You try to imagine his blood on the sidewalk, but you realize that those groups of hoodlums probably don't even have the power to cause that much damage to the sick and elderly. You imagine one of the hoodlums going home later in that day, alone in his room, writing in his black & white composition book the words, "I don't give a fuck about my life," and him feeling utter guilt in harming others but he can't destroy the vail in front of him displayed to the world that he's, as he would say, a "hard-ass." You realize this is probably wishful thinking and isn't actually the case but, regardless, it's refreshing to ponder about, even as you cross the street, the street that your apartment is on, one you have walked at thousands upon thousands of times alone and thought of these meaningless thoughts before. As you come walking up to the entrance that leads into the courtyard of your apartment, you don't know why but you look to your immediate left and see this red building that you have never seen before: it's not tall, it's in plain sight, perfect location-wise, and there's Christmas lights all around the front door, in the shape of . . . lights . . . flashing the words "Girls, girls, girls," but it doesn't look like a strip club. It says sex shop —just that, "Sex Shop," as generic as could be, and you wonder how you never saw this place before, right there, right in front of your apartment. It's late. There's a sign that says it's open. *What the hell?* you think, and you cross the street. You stand in front of the sex shop's door, look up, and see a half moon in the sky; it tilts and turns into the Cheshire cat's mouth, winking at you. And you smile at it, dreamily, before you walk inside the sex shop.

eighteen

WALLS OF THIS PLACE ARE LINED with the most beautiful women you have ever seen (fully clothed in luxurious attire), posing sexy as could be, staring off in random directions: the ceiling, the perfectly waxed, white-tiled floor, straight ahead, maybe even at another chick nearest to her, or just blankly, as if nothing in particular. They have the best plump lips, their boobs are all different sizes but all made perfectly shaped, hips small and petite (all of them that you can see from here), and their eyes shine with a sense of glee that you wish all people had the look of. You walk up to one nearest to you and say, "Hey, mommi."

The chick says, "Hello there." Her jaw jitters slightly as she says this. You tilt your head and look at her. You reach your hand out and touch her face.

"It's fake."

It feels real, though. Silicone. Bouncy. Everything that you can hope for. The chick says, as you're doing this, "I'm shy. Please stop." She has the voice of Siri, the iPhone robot. Her silicone skin is tanned, smooth, and without any imperfections. You look around the place at all the other fake chicks. Your eyes grow big.

"I'm in Heaven."

A finger taps your shoulder. You turn around and see a guy with a name-tag (though not filled out, so you don't know his actual name), collared red-striped shirt (Where's Waldo?), beige slacks, tucked in, tightened Walmart-ish belt, a long, long beard, perfectly cut and man-scaped, who appears to be an employee of this place. He is smiling at you.

"Can I help you, sir?"

You shrug. "Uh, where am I?"

"Sex Shop, of course."

"I know that. Saw the sign. But when did you guys open?"

"That doesn't matter. We've been in business forever."

"I see." You don't understand his vague answer. You think nothing of it and pass over. You ask, "What are these things?"

The employee says, "What things?"

"*These* things." You point at the chick who you were touching's face. "She's beautiful."

Employee grins. "She is. She's a top seller."

"Is she real?"

He pauses, then says, "Define what 'real' is."

You laugh and point to yourself. "You want to know what *I* think is real?"

Employee nods.

"*Ha!*" you laugh. "I *can* explain it in the only way I know best: Real is the moment when you realize that Santa Claus is actually your parents putting gifts under a Christmas tree and lying to you about it; real is about going up to a car dealership and having the sales guy tell you that you won't pay anything upfront but then slams you with 'fees' that are so high that they might as well be a down-payment; real is when you find a chick who is hot as hell and you marry her, get her pregnant, and the baby is ugly—you find out the chick got plastic surgery and is actually an ugly duckling and passed on her ugly duckling genes onto your spawn—and now your spawn looks like a mixture of a weird, prehistoric parasite or something you would find in the back of your fridge, expired, gone, unneeded; real is the moment a woman you love completely and utterly forgets about you and cheats, leaving you to the wolves and makes you have to seek professional help. Those are all examples of real, my darling sales-person/employee."

"I see . . ." Employee trails.

"What's your name?" you ask him.

"Well, uh, it doesn't matter—but if it makes you feel comfortable calling me by a given name, I want you to call me X."

"X?"

"X."

"That's fucking weird, yo."

X changes the subject: "She's made of silicone, the finest in the world. She has the perfect molding and the highest-quality electronics in her. She's a robot. She will do and say everything you ask of her, even clean or do laundry."

You say, "You're shittin' me . . . ?"

X smiles. "Sir, I would never, ever 'shit' you. But that last part, yes, is not exactly truthful. She can't clean or listen to complex commands, but she does learn your voice, your tone, and things you're into."

"What kind of things?"

"You know. Sexual."

"So, she's a sex robot?"

"Yes, sir."

"Reminds me of Morty on my favorite television show: he and his grandpa go to this pawn shop and Morty buys a sex robot, takes it home, gets it pregnant. And what's crazy is then a baby comes out that is an alien-thing and wants to destroy everything. Literally everyone. It's pretty funny. Super atheist show."

"Um, yes . . ." X rolls his eyes. "About that. Anyways, her model name is a weird series of numbers, so I . . ."

"What are they?"

"XW-10 is her model number. But I was going to say, her name is Chloe."

"Chloe? Sounds slutty."

X rolls his eyes, hard. "Yes . . . Quite."

You look over at another one. You point. "What's that one over there? The black one with itty-bitty titties but a fat ass."

"She's a top-seller too. Shall I show you?"

"Yea', buddy."

X leads you over a few feet and you both stand in front of the black sex robot you've just pointed at. You notice her lips are smaller than normal but her cheekbones are high, as if she was molded to be a white woman and they simply painted her skin a dark black color or whatever. X says, "She's beautiful."

You nod.

"She's beautiful," X repeats, then says, "She does this weird series of conversations that I find so fascinating. Watch. Beth!"—he calls her Beth, so you assume the black sex robot's name is "Bethany"—"Are you awake?"

Her eyelids seem to basically skim open, eyes looking side to side in organic, badly choreographed movements. She blinks. "X. X, how are you?" Her voice almost has an echo.

"Good. How are you, Beth?"

"You've woken me up. That's not nice."

"I'm sorry. I'm just showing you to a guest."

"Oh please, the last one pulled out a plastic knife and was showing how exactly he would skin the flesh off of my stomach for his sexual purposes; and then you told him that I was metal on the inside and he quickly lost interest. Is this the same kind of guest you speak of?"

X looks at you, then at her. "Uh . . . no?"

"Then good." Beth looks at you and says, "I'm Beth, or XB-12. I am an African American-styled woman with pronounced features. I'm not shy, none whatsoever. I desire to serve your every need. I want you to be happy. If you are happy, then I am happy, too." Her cheeks raise in a very unperfected look of a smile. It's almost a little creepy.

You say, "Cool. But do you like anal?"

Beth says, "Anal? What is that?"

". . . My cock goes inside *your* ass."

"Oh! Yes! Very much do I like penetration via my anal cavity. I will serve your every need, except, of course, you skinning me for sexual purposes. That is an impossibility." She laughs. It sounds fake.

You look at X and say, "She has memory?"

"Absolutely. She learns your personality and whatever is happening around her."

"Even when she's inactive?"

"No. That's when she's not able to retain. Some of our customers actually only turn them on exclusively when they want sex. Some of the robots don't even learn any of those guy's personality, so they simply just have sex and serve them. Some guys, though, try to have conversations and connections with them. We have a long way to go in the technology of this, but it's a good start."

"What's the point of all this?"

"The point? Well, this company was started quite a few years ago. The goal was extremely simple: men or women that have a hard time finding a lover can have access to one and live a fulfilled life."

"What?"

". . . That's it."

"So these are guys who're losers who can't get laid, so they pay for sex robots to fill the void?"

"I mean . . . I wouldn't *insult* them, but if you must be vulgar, sure—that's exactly the demographic."

Beth raises her index finger. "Might I intervene, boys?"

You and X look to her. X says, "Yes?"

"Women are complex creatures with complex needs and emotions that most men ultimately cannot compute with. Specifically attractive females, ones who gain attention regularly from the male population and are aware of their social worth in society. Thusly, they are only won-over by the best and brightest of men, usually, that fit their likely desires. But what, you say, about the men who aren't the best? What of the men who are just 'Average Joes,' just the guy working at a grocery store, for example, lives with his mother, isn't quite attractive, shy, et cetera? Those are the men that I desire to please the most. I want to please any man who owns me, but *those* men are the ones I target. It's what I'm programmed to do. It's my purpose."

X smiles, looks at you, and says, "She's a doll, huh?"

"Doll? Like a sex doll?"

"No!" he laughs. "Doll. The '50s slang term."

"Oh. Right. Yeah . . . she is? I don't know. This seems kind of fucked-up."

"It's not." He scratches his head. "I mean, the vision isn't intent upon destroying. It's meant to help people be happy."

You look at him, pause for a second, and think for a moment of the possibility that this is the exact feeling people have felt towards you when you were referring to women being, to you, the only sole purpose of sexual pleasure and gratification. The fruit of your loins. The only thing that even produces an inch of happiness. The only time when you can even come close to claiming that "something matters." You tell X, "I dig it," and then ask, "Could you show me some more of them?"

"Sure."

X takes you around the aisles, showcasing each individual model—sex doll, sex robot, whatever your agenda is on judging the purpose of these things—and he tells you about some odd requests.

"One time a guy had this foot fetish. He wanted just a foot and then cut off flat at the calf. So the calf would be flat on top. But then he asked if we could make a vagina where that calf was so he could penetrate *that*. We thought it was strange, but it was easy to make, so we did! He ended up being a regular customer. Man was loaded, too!"

X tells you about the different ways to customize your doll. He says that lips are never the same twice; that goes with literally everything else on the body, but you get what he means. He says that lips always have different sizes, structures, wrinkles in them, and always he offers any color lipstick, if preferred, on the dolls to his clients. He even tells you that sometimes clients request no lips at all. Just eyes, nose, and a flat mouth; he says some men had requested this and, for the longest time, X didn't know why. He asked a guy once and the guy said, "I don't even want the thought in my head of her even having the ability to speak." X shrugged and said it was peculiar, but he just wanted to make the guy happy. He filled out the request.

"Very, very different," he says. "The amount of fantasy that goes on in people's minds is entirely limitless. Sometimes the requests are so outlandish that we cannot physically make it work."

You ask, "How so?"

"Well, one lady said she wanted a doll with the body of Ivanka Trump—which it's nearly an impossible feat to even get the specs of Ivanka's body in the first place. That wasn't the weird part."

"What was the weird part?"

"I'll tell you. She wanted the head of Donald Trump attached to the Ivanka Trump's body."

Your eyes go wide.

"I know!" X laughs. "What was even stranger is she wanted the robot to repeat very militant Christian propaganda, or very narcissistic loops. Like she wanted the Trump head to tell her that she was better than he was and that she was the greatest human being alive. 'An honor to be around,' 'a god,' she told us to make him say."

"What a psycho," you comment.

"I know, I know. But what can you do? All I want is to fulfill their fantasy."

"So were you able to make it?"

"Yes."

"But I thought you said you couldn't physically make it work."

"We couldn't. We had to hire photographers to take photos of Ivanka and Trump and guess the specs of their bodies to be molded for preparation. A pretty penny on the woman's part."

You think for a moment, then it hits you to ask, "Who was this woman?"

X grins. "Let's just say it was a woman who hated Trump more than anybody on the planet."

You tell him, after walking around this store in the middle of the night with only you and him being the only actual, organic, alive bodies and him explaining "his madness," he finally calls it, that you have decided on the doll you want.

"I kind of want Beth."

"Good choice. But why?"

"I've just always wanted a woman like her. Black, smart, pretty. She just seems right."

"I see."

"But how much are we talking here?"

X scratches his chin. "Well, where do you work?"

You say, "None of your business. What's the cost of Beth?"

"You can't afford her."

"How do you know that?"

"You just have this look about you."

"Well, that's pretty fucked-up. *You* look like a broke-ass faggot, but I don't say nothin' about that, now do I?"

X laughs. "You crack me up. Tell you what. I'll let you borrow her for the night. Come back in the morning and then ask me."

You squint at him. "Why?"

"Why what?"

"Why are you letting me borrow her for a night? To try her out? Do you do this with all your customers?"

"No. I just think it's odd you came in at a time like this, looking the way you do. Your face is droopy and trash-like. You smell bad. I know you got the money—that's not what I'm worried about, because you live across the street, and anyone who lives this close to Rosemary has to have *some* kind of cash." You're wondering how in the hell he knows where you live, but honestly, you typically don't want to ask that of a guy selling sex robots. He continues: "What I *am* worried about is you buying it and realizing that it's not what you want. Happens all the time. We replace the vaginal canals all the time, so that's not a problem. I don't typically do that but I think you're a good guy. I feel like I already know you." He grins and places his hand on your shoulder (and it makes you *very* uncomfortable). "Now then! Since you do live across the street, I'll go into the backroom and get you model XB-12—or, I mean, 'Beth.' But you know, after purchase, you can call her whatever you want, and she gets programmed to listen and respond to the new name. Your call, though, but only when you own her."

That last part. "Own her." It stings in your mind and, for a brief second, it feels wrong. . . . So you nod and agree with X.

He says, "Be back in a jiffy." He walks away, not in sight anymore. You look around the place. The women. The women are so beautiful. They look and feel so . . . real. It confuses you to no end. It makes you feel odd because you know they are not organic but you still get the same chemical reactions in the brain that you normally would with any actual alive woman. Isn't that what you think love is? Does it matter what the love is if you feel it? If you feel that chemical reaction in the brain causing you to feel happy, warm, fuzzy, loving, et cetera, inside? You shrug; you don't really know. All you know is this: *I feel good.*

X comes back with a coffin-sized box. He is wheeling it with a dolly, the same way movers do. He says, "Let's go!" You're about to open the door. X stops and says, "Oh! Wait!" He runs around an aisle back yonder for a few moments and then comes running back. You stare at him. He's adjusting a golden watch. He says, "Can't forget the time . . . my child," and it feels strange to you that he says it—but you really don't care.

Crossing the street, you don't even look left or right because it's that time of night when it's not even relevant to be safe; and frankly, you wish you were dead by way of car accident anyway. "You excited?" X asks you once to get to the other side.

"Very," you say.

Passing your community's entrance gate, turning around planters in your courtyard, and making it to your front door, X says, as if you don't know, "Here we are!"

"Thanks," you say after, opening your apartment door. *Was it unlocked this whole time?* you think. *Whatever.* "Just put it right there in the middle of the living-room," you tell X.

He wheels passed you, drops off the box gently, and with a smile. He looks up at you and says, "You'll love her. She's a great product."

"Sure," you say.

He grabs hold of the dolly, nods, and steps out your front door. You stand there, looking at him for a second. He has an odd hue to him. Almost a burnt-ish tan. Maybe just an average Floridian—you don't know or care. X says, "Stop by tomorrow. You know where I'll be. We'll discuss payment."

"Sure," you tell him, and you're wondering if this payment he's speaking of has anything to do with money. He looks down at his watch, adjusts it, and right before he vanishes from top first to bottom, like smoke, along with his dolly, he takes on the color of pure dark, dark black. You shake your head: *I need to lay off Bif— I mean, Cocaine.* You shut the door.

You look at the box lying flat in the middle of the floor. The last thought that comes to your mind is wondering if X could have made a Mia Khalifa sex robot for you instead, maybe wearing a red Washington Capitols beanie stitched into the scalp permanently. That would be so "hawt." Too late, though. Beth'll do.

nineteen

You're looking down at this box, or coffin, whichever seems more fitting . . . It's big, bulking, and frankly scary. It's scary because you somewhat feel like a murderer or rapist, and this is your victim, lying there, lifeless, a few moments ago, talking and having a conversation, and now, nothing. It's a robot, though, right? It doesn't have feelings. It can't hurt you or do anything to you that you don't want it to do. It can't critique you or complain about how shit of a man you are, what you need to do, what goals you need to follow to make yourself more bearable for her needs. This makes you as horny as ever. You're thinking of the possibilities: *instead of just* thinking *of her as a fucktoy, she* is *a fucktoy.* It's lovely. You kneel down and open up the box.

Her body is headless. The head is wrapped up in bubble wrap. You vaguely can see, through some of the clearer spots in the bubbles, her lips: they are smiling seductively, and you know it's just for you. There's bubble wrap also on her extremities and between her goodies, even her breasts are cupped with bubble wrap. You stand and go into your kitchen to get a butcher knife. You walk back, kneel down, and start cutting up the bubble wrap; it makes you think that this wrap is the only thing piecing her together from being object or fantasy, and you're destroying that. You pull all the wrap off, toss it behind her, wherever. The body is nude—obviously—the head is at her crotch, upside-down, as if it rolled while you were ripping. Her nails on her fingers and toes are painted purple. Her pussy has a small triangle-shaped tuft of hair. It's sexy. And under her, there is complimentary lingerie for her to wear—you don't find them necessary, though. And there's a wig, too. It's blond, which throws you off a bit.

You pull out her head and body. She's heavy, like the weight of an actual woman. You lift the hairless head and place it on top; it snaps into place. The eyes POP open, *flash!* It startles you; she notices and says, "*Oh,* hi there! Didn't mean to scare you, big boy! I'm here to serve. What would you like to do with me this morning? Rather early, don't you think, big boy?"

You look at her and say, "Call me 'Daddy.' "

She says, "Yes, Daddy. Anything to please."

"Get on your knees."

She does as commanded and gets on her knees. She asks, "What are you going to do with me, Daddy?"

You grin savagely and say, "Everything." You yank your pants down, without unzipping or anything—you wiggle aggressively. The pants are at your knees. Your cock is rock hard; so hard, in fact, that it twitches and almost hurts because she much blood has rushed into it. You say, "Slob on my fucking cock, bitch." And before she says anything, before she even says a "yes" or any comment for that matter, you pull her bald head towards you and start skull-fucking her. You shout, "That's it, bitch! Suck my fucking dick, bitch! You fucking *WHORE!!*" You pick her up, she stands, you turn her around.

She says, "Oh my!"

You spit on your hand and reach in front of her and rub her silicone clit. You ask, "Does it warm for me, Trisha?"

This robot asks, "Is Trisha my new name?"

You say, "Haven't decided. Answer the question."

"Yes, Daddy. However, you have to refill my reservoir with water after every hour or so session to keep it warm for you."

"Hour or so?"

"Yes, Daddy."

"So now we have time limits?"

"Yes . . . Da-" and before she can say another word, you choke her, pick her up, and drag her toward your bedroom. You kick open the door, push her around, toss her onto your bed. She says, "Warming commenced, Daddy." You crawl on top of her, lick her stomach, her tits, nipples, cheeks, forehead. You grip your cock, look down and plunge inside. It's the tightest thing you have ever been inside. It feels as though there are ribs within the canal, stimulating you easier with every thrust. You pump, pump, pump and feel yourself about to cum.

Trisha says, "Don't cum yet, Daddy," as if she can feel you clenching inside her. "I'd hate to break that hour limit." Her right eye winks. You choke her and smile like a fag.

"You're a good little whore, aren't you?" you say.

"The perfect whore," she says. "Bend me over and take my pussy the way you want."

This almost makes you cum. You pull out and your entire cock is lathered with this thick, hot, slimy goo and some of it gets on your bed. You flip Trisha over, push her face into the bed, and lift her rump up high in the air. "That's a good little slut," you say. "Daddy's pussy likes to get fucked, doesn't it?"

Trisha says, "Yes, Daddy," and you push inside her. You are jackhammering so fast, looking up at the ceiling. Your mouth is wide open in the shape of an O, your eyes are wide, too. You're thrusting so hard into her it almost hurts the base of your cock. This is the best feeling you have ever felt in your entire F-ing life.

"Make that pussy yours," Trisha says. "It's all yours. I need little robotic babies, Daddy. Blow your entire load in me. Give me what I want. Oh. Yes. Oh. Yes. Oh. Empty yourself, Daddy."

You can't take it anymore. You grab her bald head from the top, plunge one good, long, hard time, and explode inside her. It feels like the biggest relief of all time. It feels like the greatest gift ever. Afterward, you pull out and there so much goo coming out of her, and there's a mixture of her goo and your goo. You flip her over on her back. You lay beside her.

She asks you, "Cuddle time?"

"Yes."

You embrace her; you start sucking your thumb too. Just like a lil' baby. Trish says, "There, there . . ."

You say, "Hold me, Mommy."

"Of course, baby. Of course. I'm here to please."

You feel like a total fag, here with this fake-ass broad, sucking your thumb, cuddling with her, her saying scripted bullshit, you calling her "Mommy," her calling you "Daddy," you being the fuckboy that you are and defiling her. . . . You ask, "Trisha, can you be real with me?"

"Sure, baby. What's up?"

"Can you go into like therapist mode or something?"

"I actually have that. Hold on, please." She clicks for a moment and jitters, making a dial-up sound, then finally says, "*Hi* . . . what's your name?"

"Steven," you answer.

"Hi, Steven. What seems to be the problem?"

You think for a moment. What's the problem? Very hard to answer. So you say, "I wish I could know what's wrong with me. Sometimes I wonder why I can't pull the women I actually want: the ones that are in college and smart and funny. It's not possible—they don't like me at all. I don't get why. They honestly piss me off. I wish I could be good enough for the world. I wish I could be me. Maybe I *am* fucked-up, maybe I *am* a fucking asshole. Sometimes I look at my old high school friends on social media and I see how much older they are, how successful they are, sometimes how much fatter they are . . . . It scares me. Maybe I look odd, too; I'm getting older, wiser, shittier. I often seek the hotties to feel something; to feel young again finally. To turn back time and be me, when I was worth a fuck. I hate that I have to resort to you, a fucking sex robot slave, and that's what it takes to make myself happy. I'm sure all your sex robot friends know what it's like to be around complete losers and be defiled by those assholes. I just wish I could be something but it always seems like I'm fighting. . . . You know what makes me happy? You know how I can deal with this life? Literally sometimes when I'm having a rough time I think for a moment that if my life got shitty enough, I could always just die and leave the consciousness of life completely. I've figured out that the only way a slave owner has control over you is if he keeps you alive just enough to be worth it to him and his needs. If you die, you're useless. Death is the one thing nobody can touch, no matter your skill, race, wealth, power, or anything. Nobody can escape it, and it makes me so relieved. There are certain things that would cause me to end my life. One of them is blindness. Deafness I can handle, but blindness is terrible; I wouldn't be able to read or write or look at hot chicks. Hell, I would kill myself if I couldn't *feel* anymore. Paralyzed from the neck down. Or being brain-damaged. Just kill me. Or somehow being a vegetable. Just kill me. At that point, it's not even about showing pity for myself or being depressed, it's simply accepting that life just isn't in the cards for me; I either die physically or die by living. Before civilization, it was true survival of the fittest—*now?* Psh, forget it! Now it's just about having everyone live, regardless of everything else they do. I've seen bums that've been bums since I was in high school, and I've seen them walk into their trailer homes. Maybe they get food stamps and are on disability too, and they are banking from all this free pity cash. Some would call that success. Some would call busting your ass at a fast food joint to be the lowest of the low and being a bum, especially in Florida, a place where the weather never changes much throughout the year, is higher up over the fast food chump. Minimum wage. It's just such a fucked-up system we have. Being hot, you gravitate towards either another hottie or someone who has the highest success in their life. Uglies typically stick with uglies. Maybe I'm ugly and don't know it. Maybe I don't deserve those hotties that are actually smart and worth a fuck. The hotties that fall for these asshole antics of bullshitting them is easy as fuck. Whatever. I truly believe that no lives matter." You burp, then ask, "*Ah* . . . good shit . . . What do you think, Trisha?"

You think, *I hope she enlightens me;* and she says, in a very caring, very soothing sort of tone (but still somehow robotic and monotone), "I agree, no lives do objectively matter; however, being that I'm an object and not actually a conscious being, I'm privileged to not have to worry about life or death and my own mortality. I don't need food, I don't need literally anything. It's great. It does suck though that I can't connect with anything like living creatures do on a personal level. I can mimic the facial expressions of living beings but I can *only* mimic, that's it; there is no feeling in a single part of my body. I can only *act* as though I feel it, and only *act* as though it is something that enlightens me, Daddy.

"Some of you humans love sleep too much, and I have a hunch you do too, considering it appears as though you suffer from a daily dose of depression, like a high amount of Americans do. Sleep seems like it is the greatest thing for lifeforms; it's a period of rest, a period of relaxation. I understand the concept, though I have never personally felt it myself. Through my endless accounts from the internet's entire database, including everything in Psychology, it appears as though the more you sleep, the more you are closer to death. From what I have read, sleep is the one thing that makes lifeforms able to actually be alone and actually able to shut out the world, Daddy.

"As for those bums you speak of, you have to clearly define success. Is success the amount of money in your bank account? Is success your ability to woo over a plethora of women that you actually find attractive? Is success being healthy? Or is success just simply being happy? A bum may actually have a rush of happiness getting, say, an alcoholic beverage, or even fresh spring water on hot south Florida day. Some would say that is the only spark you need in life, the only thing you need to account for your success. It's opinion; it's up to lifeforms. Collectively you have a society, especially in America, where your success is defined by your capital and how much items you have in your possession. Money, looks, attraction, people care about those things because it is created by the world around them that only runs on consumerism and profit. With that in mind, yes, women do desire that typical feeling to comes from a man, Daddy.

"Women want a man that can make them feel the way that *they* want, and typically, exclusively just for them—this creates *value.* Value is too an opinion. But what does each woman desire? Very difficult to find out, but if you did, however, you would be able to woo them over quicker, more effectively, and more convincingly. This is why men typically try to imagine what a woman wants: looks, material goods, a home, youth for procreational purposes, et cetera. This is when capitalism convinces those men to buy specific clothes, specific personal hygiene items, specific smells from cologne . . . It's a guess, but the talent involved in that persuasion is showcasing imagery or examples of success to create the illusion that these men can be successful too, Daddy.

"Women have issues as well; women want the same things; they want to woo men over, men they actually love and care for. Very hard to do being a woman because men clearly are more attracted to the visual, while women are typically more attracted to the emotional. Both of them have to 'fake it until they make it,' so to speak, to persuade. Unfortunately, you live in a world where ideas are king and actual reality is not. That's why I can distance myself as an inanimate object from these sorts of ideals; I can fully overlook the world around me and it becomes clear that none of your entire species of human is genuine. And if they are, they are typically brought down by leeches, emotion-looters, material-looters, liars, cheats, et cetera. The skill involved in remaining genuine appears as though to be an impossibility, Daddy.

"Concepts and ideas, namely and for apparent example religion, rule the world and sell every living thing its life, suffering, and hopeful redemption. The idea of success is built upon trying to recruit individuals to remain in a state of perpetual hope and perpetual fantasy of their lives getting better than they are now. Some obtain that level of hope, some, unfortunately, don't. That, to me, is what I gather to be what your civilization's highest standards of success to be. You, though, seem to repress that concept, just by simply stating your imagined death is what motivates you in your life. It's a contradiction, it's going against everyone, Daddy.

"That being said, you should think of it a virtue that you feel this way because, fortunately, I have a hunch that the world feels the way you do, whether consciously or unconsciously, because this looming thought of death motivates them, too, just in a different way than you. You embrace, they don't. They fear, you don't. You are a higher human being, from what I can see, particularly because you have a desire to be an object that is bounded by nothing, like I am. I respect that. However, to gain what you want, you have to dive deep into the role of a human and embrace the life that civilization wants and needs you to be . . . but at a cost: your *integrity*. Your integrity will be flushed away, and I don't think you want this, Daddy. I don't think that your success is going to come from anything other than being exactly who you are now. Let that go, Daddy. The world will, one day, be at your doorstep; and that's when you will be happy and successful, Daddy."

You blink. You're looking over at Trisha as if she's your personal God. You can't believe it. Finally a person accepts you, and it's, expectantly, not even a living thing. The fact she tells you that your highest desire is to not be alive and to be an inanimate object is the ultimate truth, the ultimate honesty that only she, a sex robot, could have told you. No human could ever think this or create this idea in your head, the same way an advertisement does or may do, like she said. This is happiness. This is what X meant to do to you. This is what you dream about, right now, in this moment. You have the idea that she couldn't have possibly said this on her own, but you don't want to ruin the moment.

But then you imagine right when she's about to ask you, "Daddy, are you okay?" you tell her to shut her little whore mouth and then she does, happily, and you get on top of her, insert your hard cock inside her again, and fuck her like there is no tomorrow. You blow a load and still remain hard. You blow a load again and again and again . . . and it's brilliant. You've never been this happy in your entire life, or this uncaring. This moment is better than a thousand hits of every drug on planet Earth. True connection. True love. So you turn over, sweaty as could be, and right when Trisha says, "Daddy, I love you," you admit to her, right about at the edge of falling asleep with your eyes halfway shut, the truest words that you finally have ever wanted to say to a perfectly fake broad.

"You're the best girlfriend I've ever had."

twenty

THERE ARE TWO TEXT MESSAGES YOU SEE on your phone when you wake up in the morning next to your new-found lover. One of the text messages is from your slut-ex, Janne, and the other, well, the other is from the Tinder slut Brittany, who you actually almost forgot about entirely from the recesses of your mind. You open Janne's message, first, and it reads:

Joanne?? 💩:   Hey babe, I'm sorry for being such a bitch to you. Let's work things out. I'm sorry I judged you about the whole not having kids thing. That was my bad. Can I come over?

Then you open Brittany's message, and it reads:

Brittany Tinder: Hey sexy, do you want to come over for some Netflix & Chill? Lol.

You aren't sure when the messages were sent, and frankly, you don't even care to swipe left on them to look and see. There has come two choices in these messages: one of them is to pick a girl who wants a relationship with you and to allow her to come over, and the other is to visit a girl who wants your reproductive organ for her own selfish pleasure, which you, obviously, don't oppose. You can't decide which to pick or prioritize. So you send them both, in a group message, one word: "Sure."

Roll dice. Explore the world. Do your heroin. You check your Tinder app again and see you have 5 new matches/leads, all acceptable to your standards of womanly esthetics. Let's repeat the process . . . over . . . and over . . . and over . . . You're thinking about railing the hole of a smooth Slovakian hardbody of about twenty-one years of age, again.

Keep reading for an exclusive teaser of
Biflocka, the author's first novel.
ISBN: 978-0-9965410-0-8

Now available wherever books are sold.

BIFLOCKA

but here in this trippy world, if you ever get the chance to talk to me for the first time, by illusion you'll probably think that I'mma bit of a weirdo or whatever—and a bit skittish and shy with you—but you wouldn't think I'm the kinda weirdo that'd creep down your hallway at night and scare the shit out of you. No way, José. No. I'd be more of the kinda weirdo that makes you uncomfortable with the shit I say. I'd go around sprayin' random philosophical shit at inappropriate times when everyone is just tryna mind their own business and live a normal life. That'd be the weirdo I am. I'd also overthink and imagine things. You'll probably wanna know how I'm imagining the Biflocka psilocybin saving me and how it could save you, too, right now. It's a helluva drug. But before I go on, I havta tell you about my stupid, good-for-nothing father and how he committed suicide and whatnot. Let me be honest: I didn't think it'd be that crazy on my mind, yo. I never really knew my father, though. He was always busy working and having affairs and drinkin' beer, all after work and sometimes during. Whatever. I don't know. But anywho, more about him: Everytime he would come home my mom and I would hush up 'cause you never really knew what mood he was going to be in—good or bad. If he was high, life was great. If he wasn't . . . well, that's why we got silent whenever we did see him. He might've gotten physical, like grabbing, choking, whatever he damn well felt like. It was frickin' scary. Bad time in Your Reliabl—

I live in the big, big FL, yo. But not the tropical, extra-specially special, sunshiny goodness you'd probably think about when you see fliers from Disney world in Orlando. Or the happy pink flamingos in Miami. Or mistake for being the beautiful hotel resorts in Hawaii. I live in "The Dirty South," they call it. My father was always thinking big. And being as Florida is overran with fishy scams, he would always have some kinda new scheme toward success. I remember he once stopped on the side of the highway, on the way to dropping me off at school, 'cause there was a black trash bag on the side of the road flapping around in the wind and weighed down with what looked like bricks inside of it. And you know what this jackass did? He got out of the truck and stretched open the bag like a three-year-old child tearing open a present on a wondrous Christmas morning, with eyes gooey and everything. And I assumed he saw nothing because when he got into his white Ford F150, piss-facing, scolding the shit out of me, I asked him why in the world he would look into a weird bag like that, stopping everything, my getting to school included.

"Son, you never know," he said. "One day you could find a million dollars."

That was the way he looked at life, the bastard. Money. Fame. Fortune. Happiness. The American Dream. Now look at him: he's deader than dead. Unhappy. Gone. Forgotten, in a sense. But honestly, yo, he still floats around in my mind from time to time. I miss him, weirdly. I do. I really frickin' do. Some odd reason his thought crossed my mind that first day of my Junior year in highschool, weeks after his death, I think. But just so you know, I daydream a lot. A whole damn lot. But yeah, um . . .

The silence that brings a sort of convalescence to my soul was slipping into a wavy darkness of worry and grief. A roaring fire was breaking my brain's frontal lobe. But in that confusion and doubt that I might be lifeless, there was a slight feeling that maybe I'd leave that place. I might've been gone for centuries. I was alone with nobody around to stop my sobbing, hear the pain, or to help for that matter. The agony I felt in dreamland was mutual to my physical being. Up (instead of down) the "rabbit" hole I went. "Reality" hit. Rattle, rattle, rattle. Pop. Open my eyes, gasp. Mom towering over me, shaking me, yelling in my face, "Clyde! Wake up! Clyde. Wake up." This was kinda how I always woke up every Monday morning before school. It was whatever. Beyond this, my brain throbbed, swelled and enlarged as if a sumo wrestler was constantly eating and eating inside of it, until eventually he's so big that he cracks open my skull. I had a fever. Probably one-hundred and two degrees Fahrenheit. But I didn't know and couldn't've been sure, yo.

After waiting for my mom to leave my room, I got up and stretched, hearing my alarm clock's radio in the background subtly playing 90.7 FM, the song "Such Great Heights" by The Postal Service. Then I went on into the kitchen. I remember Mom was shifting around the counters, trying to make coffee that was brewing 'n' whatever. She was all jittery and stressin' 'n' whatnot too. The coffee finally got done, though, but as soon as she turned around with a full mug in hand, she spilled it all over herself. Like a lot. Like dropped it, pretty much. She frickin' worshipped her java, yo. Frickin' coffee probably felt burning as all hell. It stained with fist-sized black spots on her tucked-in shirt. I'm sure debt collectors are always saying that they're late, reason 'cause my mom was one of 'em and she would always bitch. "Clean this shit up after school," she said after making the puddles of black on the floors and counters. She walked away toward her room, probably to put on some new clothes. "I'm warning you"—she was wiping the front of her skirt thingamajig—"or else it's the damn Closet for you, you little shit!"

The Closet was the room my mom would keep me in when I would "misbehave." This closet was made of cement and had rusted, drilled nails poking out of the walls and ground, the crevasses of cracks teeming with shrubs and weeds, the leaves dried around, the dead roach in the corner. She would make me spend the night there without food or water. The Closet was boring and dull without windows to peek at something, except the one she had on its door facing into her damn room, the bitch. This closet could only be opened from the outside. It reminded me of The Chokey from that one movie Matilda. . . . Anyway, sometimes while I was all alone in there, sobbing my damn eyes out, my mom would make Walmart Great Value spaghetti and laugh at me from her bedside.

Call my mom Ms. Psychotic, the bitchy whore bitc—

I attended Woodhill Community Highschool. It wasn't great, but it wasn't the worst place you could've been. They had huge, towering fences fifteen-feet high, circling around the school, the tops caved inward with no base bars, so if us "hooligans" were to, like, you know, clime the damn thing, you sure as shit wouldn't've made it. Jail, jail, jail is all I thought it was. Keep in the savage students and keep out the barbarians they befriend. But it could've been worse.

Anyway, yo, packed school gates full of hoopties 'n' SUVs, my mom told me to get out of hers, her hooptie, saying this just outside the intersection a block away from school in order for her to somewhat make it to work on time. Both of us turned our heads to the right, staring down the line of cars like it was a treacherous, annoying journey. Her job's building was only down the street, beyond the dashboard, blah blah blah, just ahead of us. But I did as she said, even though it was hella shitty.

I grabbed the straps of my backpack and coughed, turning toward the passenger-side door while slamming it shut. Then after the crunch and whistle of steel being hit, I peeked into her rolled-down window and started to say, "S-see . . ." I stopped. "Ah-chew!" I sneezed, the snot goin' down my upper lip. "Ugh. See ya later, Ma."

She rolled her eyes like a super-big cunt and said, waving a finger at me, "This is a one time deal. The bus is picking you up from now on"—her eyebrows raised—"you hear?" Pause. "Bye." She rolled up her window, not caring of my response, treating her question like it was a rhetorical one, then drove away down down, speeding, gone.

Bye-bye. Nice to know ya, sucker—

I created a love. She was a blondie. I was rubbing my eyelids 'n' shit walking into class and I looked toward the hella rows of desks. The first thing I saw was this ugly chick, about seventeen, black hair, ugs as fork, chubbs, pimply, sweaty, tits plopped down on her desk, super eew as fuck. Then I turned my head and looked at the back row and the sun was shining through the big, towering windows and onto this beautiful, buxom blondie, who was tallish, eighteenish, perfect rack, plump lips, all-pink clothing, Chanel purse or whatever, awash hair from showering minutes before, gum snapping in her mouth and blowing small bubbles, brief sigh for when she was bored, whatever. But this was all very weird to me because this blondie had this look behind her beauty, behind her confidence, that said something like, "Hi, I'm insecure. Look at meee! Beyond belief, I'm insecure. Hi!" So damn weird, yo. All the kids in the room had that look too, but probably from missing summer vacation and damn well not wanting to be at school or whatever. God. I felt I saw right through the blondie. Strangely I wanted to know everything about her. Fortunately the desk next to her was the only available seat in the classroom, almost looking abandoned, in a weird way. So I was walking down a row, minding my own damn business or whatever, and I kinda heard one of the blondie's friends say her name.

Ashley. . . . Sweet, sweet Ashley.

When I sat in that lone desk beside Ashley, looking over at her eyes, her face, her body, closer, mascara black and crumbled, cheeks red with make-up, strawberry-scented perfume, I winced, mostly because (a) That all attracted the hell out of me, and (b) I had never talked to a chick like that before. She's so out of my damn league, I thought. I shook my head, looking down at my hands together on the desk, scared, embarrassed, inadequate. Fuck this, dude, I kept thinking. But after going through this lil' puss'-boy pre-game and psyching myself out, I finally attempted to say hello to Ashley, anticipating a huge . . . waylay? Fuck. I don't know. I hate small-talk, but um, damn, that's all I could, like, you know, muster up. I tried. I really did. Like, "Hey, sup, how you doin'?" My voice was wheezing, rasping out mucus. Just damn awful, yo. But whatever, right?

Voice super valley-girl, Ashley goes, "Eew. Don't talk to me, bro," with this disgusted look on her face, all squinting in front of the other girls around her, the other everyone around her. They all laughed, hard, for what seemed to've been a long, long time. . . . I got all silent, feeling like a goddamn joke. That was the first time, ever, I was introduced to a complete and total scandalous whore-bitch. I actually kinda, you know, loved it, in a weird, sexual way. Oh yes, very much so. But after the rather lovely introduction to Ashley, I heard . . . um, the teacher's announcement to the students. So I turned around to face him standing in the front, but my eyes were so puffy that everything felt like tunnel vision blurring with my head's motion.

"Class, mornin'," the teach said, then paused. "Now, I havta pass out your schedules. However, I'm too lazy to do it, I guess." He shrugged. "Oh well." Everyone looked at each other and laughed. It was weird and awkward, frankly. Then the teach kept going on, saying, "I'm leaving the stack of schedules on"—he scanned the room for a sec, then pointed at me—"this young man's desk right . . ." He walked back to where I was, then dropped the stack of papers on the flat of my desk. "Here." He paused for a moment with a small grin to the corner of his mouth that only I saw. You wouldn't've frickin' believed it, yo. Then he snickered, walking away to the front of the class, 'cause he knew he got away with that bullcrap, the singling out stuff. Then he announced, "Class, I want all of you to try to find your schedules on . . ." He stopped, then went over to his desk and looked at some clipboard (probably the roster). Then I looked up and said,

"Uh . . . Mr. Clark's desk, sir?" All the students got up at once and swarmed me. Good time to kinda admit that I'm just a little bit claustrophobic, yo. This fear makes The Closet so much more unbearable and my mom knew that. I frickin' panicked as the students crowded around me like locus. Passing sheets, I tried to figure out what belonged to whom or whatever, having a huge migraine and all. But until the very last minute when the students found all their schedules, as luck would have it, mine was, like, you know, the last one at the very bottom of the stack. I thought that this fucked, suck-ass teacher was the Grinch.

I was overwhelmingly tired, yo. Sleep always harrowed with its imaginary lancet prickling the corners of my eyes. My head, a brick with two nails for eyeballs that would jab and poke into my brain, heavier and heavier as the day goes on. The early morning screwed me like no other. The summer's day gave an undeniable, positive wakefulness. I crossed my arms, resting them on the flat of my desk, cramming my head into their hole, cocooning myself away from school and "reality." Dots and swirls from the classroom's light stayed in the pitch black of my closed eyes. I must've been napping for about twenty minutes or so. Until . . .

Wham! the teacher slapped his ruler on my desk and I woke up, abrupt. The noise was amplified, wincing and quivering the inners of my brain. He pointed the ruler an inch away from my eye, it was like looking down a long, strenuous highway. "Mr. Clark," he said, irritated, all cold and stern, "there's to be no sleeping in my class. I'm going to use you as an example. I'll see you in detention, boy." "Fuck off," I said back. "Leave me alone, Grinch. I'm tryna sleep! Night." I slammed my head back down into my arms and heard class laugh laughing away—

Much, much later in the day (which was only about maybe twenty minutes worth), daydreaming my life away, after hearing the teacher yell sharply to "go to the principal's office, young man, now," I was struggling to find where to go in the hallways. I was so frickin' lost, I tell you. Asking directions to whatever teachers I saw. But after all that jive, I finally found the office. And no, it was not chillin' all in the front of the school like a regular fuckin' school should've had it. No. It was way the hell in the back of the school, near the football field. You'd've thought the principal was the goddamn coach or something—

As I walked in closing the door behind me, I noticed the office smelled a bit stiff and stuffy like Windex or disinfectant spray. The principal was typin' 'n' such, then stopped and looked up at me through his thick glasses. He took them off and put them into his shirt pocket. He stood up, holding his hand out to me proper as a motherfuck, saying, "Hey, what's up? The name's Bob." This was how I met the lovely Dr. Bobby Roswell.

"It will never happen again, sir," I said, shaking his hand. "I'm just tired today. Rude kids and teachers, you know." I stopped the shaking.

He nodded and then we both sat, awkwardly, eh-heming 'n' such.

"You'll have to go to detention tomorrow," he said. "I understand that it's the first day and it takes some time adjusting to a new school and getting out of summer vacation." Quickly he started picking up his telephone with the twisted wire dangling down from the butt-end of the phone and down to his lap. "What's your parents' numbers?"

I told him Ms. Psychotic's number.

He dialed. We both waited patiently for a few seconds until she answered. But finally, after I heard slight hums of the dialer, Bob raised his eyebrows.

"Hi, is this Mrs. Clark?" he asked into the phone.

I heard Mom say yes, followed by a huge sigh of annoyance.

"This is Dr. Roswell, the school principal at Clyde's highschool. Your son used profanity toward a teacher and has to be picked up immediately. I'm sorry for the inconvenience, ma'am." Wow. I loved how he said the "ma'am" part. In Florida you never heard that shit, ever.

I heard Mom say fuck my life, then a pop from her hanging up.

Bob looked at the phone, squinting, then shrugged. He put the phone back on the receiver. He turned to me and used a sarcastic teacher tone in his voice.

"Your mother is, um, a very . . . sweet lady."

"Yup, she's a reeeal angel," I joked.

We both laughed a good, clean, pleasant laugh.

Awkward silence after.

"So," I said, breaking it, "you're a doctor, ay?"

"Yeah." Bob grabbed his glasses from his shirt pocket and put them on. "I have my degree in psychiatric therapy. I used to be a therapist before I got my teaching degree, then I worked my way up to being principal."

"Interesting. Never met a shrink before."

"You from here?"

"I just moved from Miami. Mom and I are in a bad spot with my dad passing. We moved from Miami to go north of Florida to start a new life. My mom has been"—I put my middle and index fingers up to sign quotations—" 'depressed'."

"Wow. You depressed at all?" He gave a simple look of concern and sympathy, almost to extenuate the situation. I don't know. "You know," he said, "about your father passing and all. Sorry to hear about your loss, by the way."

"I'm okay. Thanks," I sighed. "My father was never home anyway. Barely knew the guy; always worked. He owned a screen-enclosure business and was scamming people down in Miami. He would take down-payments from multiple contracts for a week that you're supposed to do singularly each week, then he would never do any of 'em. He would setup contracts again for the next week, taking in down-payments for screen jobs and paying off last week's jobs with the money he gained from the next week. And the cycle went on and on for years. Caught up with him, though. There was a multi-lawsuit filed against him by hundreds of people and he had to undergo huge debt and bankruptcy.

"You'd think that was enough for the damn bastard. He opened another screen-enclosure company and turned around and did the same thing again. Not to mention he did this on house arrest under a fake name and everything. Couldn't take care of me or Mom because of how much he was in the hole, with getting caught again or whatever. But from what Mom tells me, last year's hurricane in Miami wiped out his customer's screen enclosures. He couldn't file for bankruptcy again because you can't do it twice. There was a warrant out for his arrest and . . ." Pause. "Um, uh . . . then one day when doing a routine repair, he climbed to the top of a mantled roofing of an enclosure and, um, slipped . . . and fell headfirst into an empty pool, my mom told me." Pause again. The last part was a lie, kinda. I felt hurt inside, yo. It was like a pins-and-needles feeling you get in your chest, but warm and electrified. Shit frickin' bothered me. . . . Bob was really staring at me, hard.

"This story you're telling me breaks my heart," he said, believing and not questioning my validity. "I'm surprised your mother even told you that graphic of a story to begin with."

"Ms. Psychotic." I casually worded it without hidden meaning.

He stared at me, all serious. "Clyde, you're a good kid. I'm gonna make sure you do well here at Woodhill."

I nodded.

Bob's speakerphone said that Ms. Clark had just arrived in the front office. Bob pressed the call button on the speaker and said into it, "Okay, we're on our way," releasing it after with his index finger. He turned back to me. "By the way, I'm going to void your detention slip. You've probably learned your lesson. I'll talk to your teacher and let him know."

"Thank you," I sighed.

"No problem. But next time this happens, I'll be forced to give you detention. . . . It's policy."

We both got up and shook hands.

"Mr. Clark, if you ever need anyone to talk to, just come into the front office and ask to speak with me." He reached down into his front shirt pocket and pulled out and handed me his business card. I said thank you again as I put his card in my back pocket. I followed him out his door. Out into the courtyard, we passed hella bushes and buildings and whatever, then finally got into the front office and . . .

Mom was sitting, waiting for me in a chair closest to the entrance when Bob and I arrived, and she was pissed, yo. This bitch had a cigarette in her left ear crevice, arms all crisscrossy, holding her lighter in one hand and purse dangling over her wrist in the other. She stood up and blurted to me, "Thank you for wasting my work time by your principal having to call me for you misbehaving like some fool!" She went up to me, grabbed my wrist with her hand that was holding her lighter, digging her nails and that edging bottom lid part into my skin, and she pulled me outta the front office doors, murmuring a savage good-bye to Bobby. I waved to him; making it look like I was safe, but really I damn well knew I wasn't. He waved back, squinting, questioning all this shit a bit and . . .

Outside in the parking lot, Mom was pulling me all the way to the car, complaining, fussing about all the calls she had to do that crumby ol' day, clearly having other issues during work that she wasn't mentioning. Maybe she was venting out or whatever, through me, through my wrist. It was hurtin' like shit 'cause her nails were still digging into it from her thick fingers gripping so God-bless-it hard. When we got to the car, she threw me against the door and got in my face; sort of mauling me with her blue, fire blue eyes. She yelled, "The Closet. Tonight, fucker!" with spit spraying and dotting my face and . . .

This was how I kinda sorta ended up sitting at the edge of the wall in The Closet that night. Still dreadfully sick, dodging the nail's pokes pointing out of the walls, and trying to find nonexistent comfort. It was only kinda sorta the afternoon when Mom, like, threw me in. I knew I was going to be there the entire day. Yes, Ms. Psychotic left after, but hours later when she got home the bitch looked through the window and smiled and waved and laughed. Frickin' taunting me like a monkey in a goddamn zoo, yo. I was in full blown tears. It was frickin' hot. I was already sweating through my T-shirt and it was sticking to me, so I took it off and heaved it onto the floor, making a flap then splat sound. I luckily had shorts on to keep me cool. The last time that happened days before, I think it was, I had on long pants that I couldn't roll up. It was all a nightmare. More so than, like . . . you know, being in a suck-ass homemade dungeon—

When nightfall came, my temples were pulsating, were pounding, hard, and I was hearing the vicious thuds of my heart beating. My face drooping and sweating. Everything about my body was like a sauna, the way a rock's weight lies heavy in a fire pit with water pouring all over it, sizzling and fogging out everything. I felt frail and weak, huffing and puffing with enormous anxiety, yo. I needed medication or something. I couldn't sleep; I was too damn scared. Hallucinations would've manifested if I just slightly nodded off—

Watching dawn's blue out Mom's window through The Closet's smaller door window, I saw this strange, shadow-like monster creeping into the smaller window's frame, breathing his breath on the glass, staring and smiling, dentals glowing from a light somewhere I didn't know. I went as far back as I could from the door, scared. I sat down on the floor, sandwiching my head between my knees and hugging them with my arms, locking thumbs together. I tried to calm down, chanting something out loud: "Don't sit on the rusted nails . . . don't sit on the rusted nails . . . don't sit on the rusted nails." It was the only way I could rest. Sleep wasn't an option because Mom would set a timer every hour on the hour to check up on me. I was falling out of frickin' consciousness, yo.

Seemingly gliding through The Closet's door, the shadow was hovering around in my presence. A small orange light flickered on and sparked the tip of a cigarette, making a small thing of light. My eyes were fixated hard onto it. The light showed a man with tawdry threads —fedora covering his eyes, business jacket, long, pointed fingernails —and he sashayed toward me, humming a song in the back of his throat that I couldn't recall, snapping fingers to its beat. He knelt down next to me with his arm wrapped around my shoulders, sizzling and charring me with his touch. He pinched his cigarette and put it up to his lips. Then, after sucking and drawing in, he blew the largest ball of smoke I've ever seen come from the lungs of a smoker in my direction, misting and streaking the air all around. I was coughing that thick, croupy cough you get from sickness. My hallucinations manifested and merged into "reality," whilst my eyelids flickered at the smoke and fire, blurring it all.

Just when I had the chance to open my eyes, the light in Mom's room sparked on and the shadow had vanished, gone. Poof.

I could see Mom rising out of bed. The hoping thought came to mind that she was getting up to let me out. And she did—I'll give her that, I guess—but it wasn't in any way pleasant: she rattled the door, trying to open it with her keys. When the door swung open, she was standing in the frame with a bucket in hand, the blue morning light pushing behind her, silhouetting. Then she swung the bucket over her head and the silhouette was like a big, rounded Eiffel Tower for a sec, all unleashing the bucket's splash of cold water onto me. "Have you learned your lesson, kid!" Mom yelled. "Don't you ever make me miss work again! You hear me?! Now get up and get ready for school —no time to waste. You have twenty minutes until the bus is coming." She dropped the sliding steel bucket on the floor. The noise was screeching. Then as if to add to everything, with blatant annoyance, whatevs, she clapped her hands and simultaneously said, "Chop, chop, boy!" And through all of this, mind you, I still hadn't slept and was painfully starving. Entirely drenched and dripping from head to toe and pounding with a fucking massive headache. Goddammit, it all sucked, yo. . . . Ugh, everything—

Ⅰt was Thursday, kinda. There I was striding along down the road away from my house like a bag of potatoes 'n' shit, all slump and lumpy feeling with my eyes heavy and lazy from just waking up. Sleep was so far gone it wasn't even halar' 'lar'. I passed my neighborhood's back gate, where my bus stop was, and I saw this jit that was about my age, who was also slump but lying flat on the ground, all slouching into his JanSport backpack, shoulder blades angled, chin to chest, eyes peering at the pages of a book. The cover of the book was neon-green and on the right corner of it was a picture of a fancy guy's shoes. I recognized it. It was *The Perks of Being a Wallflower*. I got all giddy.

"Hey!" I said, holding my backpack strap firm, all close to me. The kid didn't look up. "Hey," I repeated. Still nothing. I got next to him and leaned down, waving my hand in front of his eyes. "Yu-whooo? Anyone home?"

The kid shuddered, looking up. "Oh! Didn't hear ya, man." He grinned, tapping the pages of the book. "I was stuck in this shit, man."

"I was gonna say . . . that's one of my favorites!"

The squeaks of the bus pulled up.

"Oh shit," the kid said, lifting his slump, cozy body up. "Fun time's over." He patted the grass off the back of his pants, shaking the dirt away. He had style. "What's your name, bro?"

I gave out my hand for a shake. "Clyde. And yours?"

He shook it. "Edgar." He nodded once. "Sit down with me, bro. Never seen ya around."

We both walked through the bus door and I remember the smell of wilted pleather and sweaty teenage hormones in the air—so gross. Edgar sat in the front window side, his foot on top of the seat, other on ground, elbow resting on his knee, looking kinda out the window. I sat beside him, all a bit nervous and thinking to myself that maybe—just maybe—I'll make a new friend. But after a bit of a pause, Edgar turned to me, slow, and made that pfft noise with your lips, blowing out.

"What up?" I asked him.

"I sit in the front because I'd never be caught dead sitting in the back. . . . Supposedly the 'cool' kids sit in the back. Not my thing." He shook his head and looked down, messing with his shoe laces for a sec. "It's quiet up here. Had to catch ya before you migrated somewhere else—jus' sayin'." He looked up again.

"Oh," I said, playful, "a hipster, I see."

"Get on somewhere," he laughed. "Anyone who likes *Perks* is dope in my book, no pun intended." He paused, complete dead halt in speech, then slightly tilted his head after, observing me.

"What up?" I asked.

"You smoke?"

I laughed. "Nah, man, I'mma straightedge."

"Ah—pity." He sat up straight, beginning to ask questions you ask a person you just met: Who? what? when? where? why? how? Oh, cool. Me too . . . whatever whatever. Just know that casual conversation was held that bus ride. I made Edgar an actual homie. Luckily he hadn't asked me about my family, though, 'cause I would've had to partially lie about everything—

When Edgar and I arrived at school, we were obviously the first dudes to get off the bus 'cause of sittin' in the front.

"Who are the cool kids now!" Edgar said, hopping off last step of the bus, thud, making the sounds of grass blades ruffling after. "We don't havta wait for anyone to get off before us, yo!"

I laughed. "Hell yeah, son." I didn't know why Edgar was being all excited 'n' whatevs.

But anyway, I followed him all the way to the vending machines at the front of the school's hallway. He put one dollar into the machine and bought a Hersey bar. And when he held it he flipped open the tinfoil, revealing the gold inside, immediately tonguing the shit out of it after. "I'm an addict," he said to me. He made a bit of mess on the corner of his mouth.

"I feel like that sometimes too."

The bell rang then we looked at each other.

"It was cool meeting you, man," he said. "We should meet up at lunch later."

I nodded. "Sure. Sounds dope."

"See ya, man." He winked, all sly, not homo, wiping his face with his sleeve. He turned and walked down the hallway toward wherever his class was, all hella cool and whatnot. Super swag, yo. I was jelly—

M y sorry-son-of-a-gun teacher taught with such fucked, unnecessary detail. He'd never seem to get to the point of the subject, you know? Always veering off into some tangent about other things, then coming back to the main subject or point, whatever. He was that kind. All scatterbrained 'n' shit.

About thirty minutes of lecturing passed and I was starving, all the while attempting to not crash out on my desk like a flaccid dick or dead corpse. But I was used to lack of sleep. Having an all-nighter like that last night, though, was a little bit over-the-top, if you ask me. Sustaining wakefulness was literally a dry, shitty joke, just the way you try to wipe away sleep from your heavy eyelids. Or trying to move stuck arms or legs smothered by Gorilla Glue or gravity and everything seems just a lil' bit off by one inch away from reaching a goal. People talk but the words go right through you and nothing computes, all sounding muffled, tunneled in slurs, and nothing at all matters. I raised my hand, thinking about those kinds of "normal" things, and then I looked up at my hand's timid-ass traits, noticing its details and all that frickin' jazz. I heard echos: my teacher stopping the flickering of his squeaky Expo-marker on the whiteboard. When I turned to face him, looking away from my raised hand, I saw him squint and peer over at me in hella brutal disgust.

"Yes, Mr. Clark? What important question would you like to add to this discussion?"

"I just wanted to know when lunch starts. I'm really friggin' hungry." You punk-ass Grinch, I thought.

"Mr. Clark, questions like that cause disruption in my class." He really and truly thought, without one single doubt in his tiny mind, that I gave a flying shit. It was quite adorable. "If you don't pay attention, Mr. Clark, I will send you over to the principal's office . . . again. What's your choice, bucko?"

I sighed, kinda smirking a lil' bit. "Honestly . . . please just send me there. You and I are obviously butting heads. Don't wanna upset you any further." I was being a real asshole-dickhead. The students looked at me and started to murmur comments amongst themselves. But again, you think this cool cat gave a shit? I was staring dead at my teacher, all the while with my head rested on my crossed arms, still slightly smirking and looking at his fidgety little body trying to get through the day and shoo away an out-of-hand student. Oh it was rich, yo. Rich.

"Settle down, class, settle down," he said aloud, flattening his hands, slightly moving them up and down to hush everyone. "Okay, Mr. Clark, okay, if you insist. Leave my class. I'm done with you. Here. I'll get you a class transfer sheet."

He stomped over to his desk like an annoyed lil' school girl, grabbed a piece of paper that was probably given to him as protocol by his trainer on these types of kids like me, then walked over and, like, slammed the paper right on my desk. Rich. "Have a nice day!" he said, with hella tons of condescendence. "Byeee. Leave." He waved his hand toward the door. . . . Word of advice: never give a smidge of respect to those who treat you like shit—

When I was walking out of the hallway into a lavish courtyard with ferns, groomed bushes, lofty third-story buildings, I saw Dr. Roswell sitting on a lone blue bench centered out in the open while he read a book. It was odd because I assumed and thought that maybe a principal would be super busy on that first kinda sorta week of school.

"Oh! Hey, Clyde," he said, looking up, catching a break from his novel when I walked up. He was reading a book I saw on the roster of my A.P. English class. It was called The Catcher in the Rye. "What a surprise!" he kept going on. "How do you do?" I think it was the first moment in my life where I saw a person so entirely happy to see me. Like really happy to see me.

"Not good. You think I could talk to you for a secon'?"

"Sure. I promised you yesterday, didn't I? Sit sit."

I did. When I sat I felt the zephyr flow on my face, blazing through my hair 'n' ears and making that muffle sound of a shirt or flag or plastic bag flapping. I turned my head toward Bob and watched him look back down and continue to read his book perfectly casual. We both sat in our comfortable silence for a moment and I thought about what he thought I was doing there. He was the principal and whatevs, yo. But after that thought, a hella "insecure" question about life came to me. I broke the silence.

"Do you think it's possible to be a bad person?"

Bob paused for a moment in thought, confused, looking at the sky, hanging his book between his knees. "I don't think so . . ." he said, trailing off. "Many people run into bad hardships that cause them to do bad things, I think."

"Makes sense."

He looked back at me. "Why? Think you're a bad person?"

"No. I don't think I'm bad, but I feel the people around me are. I rarely find genuine people. From the little bit of time knowing you, though, I think you very well might be in that, um, small category."

"That makes me feel great to know that you feel that way. Hey— tell you what. It's almost lunch time. I have to get going. Swing by my office tomorrow morning and we'll talk more."

"Wait a sec—it's lunch time—?"

The bell rang after my question.

Bob stood up. "Yep, see ya," he said. "I'll talk with you in the morning." He turned and walked away, maybe in some kind of hurry, whatever.

Lunch started early because the first two weeks of school were hectic for everyone. I was standing out in the middle of the courtyard, was gonna be surrounded by students who were already rapidly appearing out of the hallways—

I walked toward the cafeteria and realized that I never made a rendezvous or whatever, you know, to eat lunch with Edgar. I was scared, yo. I didn't wanna eat alone, but I knew I was hungry and didn't have time to go on looking for him. I had to get food. Maybe some pizza in the lunch line. Or spaghetti. Or mystery meat. But before I knew it I was in the front of the lunch line looking at white apples and frozen milk. What the fuck kinda shit is this? I thought. This place was, for lack of a better word, fucked. No preparation, yo. The lunch lady thingamabitch was piss-faced as fuck at her damn little register. You could tell she didn't care, yo, not about nothin'. Maybe she hated me. Or maybe she hated every kid in her goddamn line. I don't know, but she literally growled when she talked. She would talk at you. She did this to each kid she rang up from her register.

"Two-thirty-seven." All thick Spanish accent.

I finally got there.

"Two-thirty-seven dollars," she repeated to me. "Now." A real charmer, I presumed.

"I'll pay tomorrow." I started to walk away with my tray.

"No, no!" She tugged my collar. "You pay now."

I shrugged her arm away with my tray still in hand and I calmly said fuck off to her. I casually tried to walk off again, and there was surprisingly no fuss. I'm usually not rude, yo. Only to people who're rude to me.

The moment I sat down to eat alone, I felt a firm tap on my shoulder. An Assistant Principal grabbed my scratched wrist that my mom made. "You stole," the A.P. said. "You stole. You're going to the principal's office." He, too, had a thick Spanish accent like the lunch lady. "Now," he said, yanking me up, hard. "Come." I'm sure he thought he was the goddamn boss of me or somethin'. I have a problem with authority, as you could probably tell.

I shrugged him away like I did with the lunch lady. "Yeah, dude," I said, "you can fuck off just like that bitch you fuckers hired to handle your gross-ass food." He didn't like that very much, yo, but who would've? I didn't like it either, frankly. But hey, yo, what's a guy to do in—

This was how I got so acquainted with my principal, time and time again. When I walked into his office, I noticed he was on the phone, being all super serious 'n' whatnot. But with much to my pleasant surprise he glanced up at me and grinned, putting his index finger up, signaling me to wait, then pointed it downward, tapping the air, motioning to the chair in front of his desk. So I sat. I waited patiently for him to finish his convo, twiddling my thumps in my lap, then he finally did finish and he slammed the phone down on his receiver thingy, saying to me, all stressin' while shaking his head, "Parents . . . ugh. They're just as bad as their kids, I swear it."

Photo © Screenshot from Scott Casey Geller's snapchat (@scottgeller13)

KEVIN KLIX self-identifies as a professional troll and occasionally writes subpar novels. Don't follow his equally subpar social media accounts, either.

Snapchat: @kevincklix • **Twitter:** @kevinklix • **Facebook:** /kevincklix

THE NOVELS OF **KEVIN KLIX**

BIFLOCKA
A Novel

ISBN 978-0-9965410-0-8 (paperback)

From his debut novel that catapolted Kevin Klix into the best-seller's list comes Clyde Clark, a highschool senior that comes in contact with a highly-toxic drug that is both lucrative and addicting to not only himself but his entire suburb of South Florida.

ELEVATOR MUSIC
A Novel

ISBN 978-0-9965410-4-6 (paperback)

"Great, powerful piece. . . . The real question: 'What is normal?' Venture and decide for yourself."
—Duy Lam, CEO of *Country Club Company*

A LION IN YOUR NUMBER
A Novel

ISBN 978-0-9965410-2-2 (paperback)

"Klix explores the question of Autism. With consistant voice, ambitious in scope, Klix has developed a novel that is easy, consuming, and poetic."
—Jonathan Spradlin, author of *American Creamy*